I0713427

Snapshots

The Collected Flash Fiction of Jeff Coleman
Volume 1

Jeff Coleman

SNAPSHOTS. ©2017 Jeff Coleman.

All rights reserved under International and Pan-American Copyright Conventions. No part of this book may be reproduced in any form or by any means without express written permission from the author, except in the case of brief quotations embodied in critical reviews and certain other noncommercial uses permitted by copyright law.

Stock images used in the cover: "Artistic surreal imagine representing a window into nature at night" © Valentina Photos/Shutterstock.com; "Full moon seen with a telescope from northern emisphere - Isolated over white" © Claudio Divizia/Shutterstock.com; "Vintage or grungy of Concrete Texture Background" © Sakarin Sawasdinaka/Shutterstock.com; "Arched window in a stone wall" © Aleksey Sagitov/Shutterstock.com.

Published internationally by Pallid Visions®
PO box 5943
Buena Park, CA 90622
United States

This book is a work of fiction. Any similarity between the characters and situations within its pages and places or persons, living or dead, is unintentional and coincidental.

For more information about the author, visit his homepage:
https://blog.jeffcolemanwrites.com/

ISBN 978-1-945997-07-5 (Hardback)
ISBN 978-1-945997-08-2 (Paperback)
ISBN 978-1-945997-10-5 (E-book)

Library of Congress Control Number: 2017919486

First edition.

Contents

Acknowledgments

This book is for my wife, my parents, and my patrons. Thank you for believing in me and for your never-ending support. If you became a patron after December 13, 2017, I'm sorry I wasn't able to list you here. But know that you, too, hold a special place in my heart, and that this book wouldn't have been possible without you.

Jill Babbs
Liza Carrasco
Voni Colannino
Julia Davis
Angela Escarcega
Andi Graham
Denise LaDoux
Thom Millman
Jessica Parkko
Suzie Queen
Karen Sutton
Pat Williamson

AmySue Bortz
Janis Chandler
Jeannine Cook-Battles
Christyne Demos
Monica A. Franklin
Leah Hubbel
Melody LeBeau
Allen Morris
Robert Peirson
Ivette Rivera
Jenn Vaughn

Vickie Bracken
Anthony Colannino
Justin Cooper
Cara Eckman
Anna Garcia-Centner
Buffy Kennedy
"JonBoy" Maddron
Karen Palumar
Lisa Plante
Kim Slater
Chad Walker

Foreword

The flash fiction started as a happy accident. I had only a couple of e-books under my belt, a short story and a middle grade fantasy—and no audience to read them. What to do? I could share excerpts to show off my style, get people excited (I hope) about my writing, and (I hope again) make them want to read more. But what would happen when they reached the end of one of my books? They take a long time to write, revise, and publish, and by the time I had another one out, those who'd read my previous two titles would probably have forgotten all about me.

Well, shit.

Before I started writing books—before publishing was anywhere on my radar—I used to write short stories. And by short stories, I mean *really* short stories. Sometimes I would call them snapshots, because they were more like still frames of some specific event or character I wanted to explore in greater depth later; each would typically be a page or less in length and well below 1,000 words. I would learn later that the most correct classification for this type of writing is flash fiction.

Flash fiction was perfect for a timid writer like me. Terrified of failure, I would avoid starting longer works because I didn't want to invest all my time in producing an epic volume only to realize halfway through that it absolutely sucked. Of course, as I got older, I realized the only way to create something halfway decent was to first create a whole lot of things that sucked. But that sort of truth isn't usually accessible to the very young, so I would sit down for an hour or two at a time when everyone else had gone to bed, turn on a desk lamp, and crank out another one of my "snapshots" before turning out the light and going to bed myself.

After I started publishing and realized I needed to build an audience, the idea of flash fiction came back to me. It would be impossible to churn out a book each week, but what about a piece of flash fiction? It was the perfect format. I could explore a breadth of topics that might make good novels and novellas (a few of my flash fiction pieces have since been turned into longer stories), create something that people looked forward to on a regular basis, and present examples of my style, so that when it came time to sell a new book, there would be people waiting, eager to read it.

It took me a while to get over my perfectionism and to be willing to post something new every week that hadn't first been through my critique group and reviewed by a group of editors, but once I did, people told me how much they enjoyed my stories. And now, here I am, a few years later, with a burgeoning audience of wonderful and supportive readers.

It was never my intention to focus so much of my time on flash fiction. I wanted to write books, and I wanted people to read my books. The flash fiction was simply a means to an end. Yet now, with so many people looking forward to my weekly posts, it's become a cornerstone of my platform. A few people have even asked me for print collections of what I've posted on the blog so they can enjoy my work offline, which is one reason that I've compiled this book now.

I've done my best to categorize each story. Some categories have been given very specific labels (e.g. Childhood, Depression, and Writing), while others have been grouped according to broader criteria, generally by genre (e.g. Horror and High Fantasy.) Stories rarely fall under a single category, but I've tried to organize them anyway in the hope that it'll be easier for you to find something you're in the mood to read.

If you're one of my long-time readers, I want you to know how much your support and your enjoyment of my stories means to me. I never imagined in all my life that I'd get to touch people's hearts the way I have through fiction.

If you're a new reader, welcome! I hope you'll like what you see and decide to stay for more. If this book is the only time our paths will cross, I hope you'll get something special out of it that will stick with you as you go for a spin on this crazy ride called life.

Finally, if you're a patron, I want you to know how singularly special you are. Without you, none of this would exist. Your support, both moral and financial, has enabled me to do things I never thought possible. Thank you so much, a thousand times, THANK YOU!

One last thing before I go. You should know that most of these flash fiction pieces are available on my blog for free. You can find them at: **https://blog.jeffcolemanwrites.com** (along with many other stories that weren't completed in time to be included in this volume). I have, however, included some stories that you can only read through Patreon, so if you're not an official patron, you'll see some new pieces here.

Now, sit back and enjoy, and if you feel so inclined, shoot me an email to tell me what you think: **jeff@jeffcolemanwrites.com**. I'm looking forward to hearing from you :)

Childhood

Introduction

Childhood is a topic I explore often in my writing. Like purpose, death, and the afterlife, childhood fascinates and haunts me. It's an all-too-brief period where the heart retains its innocence, where everything is new, where magic is possible, and where dreams and reality are two sides of the same coin.

It isn't until we've grown up, thinking nothing's ever going to change except our height and our freedoms, that we appreciate how fleeting it was, and when we try to look back, to catch a glimpse of what we've lost, we discover it's like staring through the wrong end of a telescope, so distant from who and what we've become that we can no longer discern the details that were once so important to us.

When I sit down to write about childhood, that's when I peer through the wrong end of my own telescope and try to remember the boy I was long ago.

A Father's Encouragement

"Come on, son. You can do it."

"No, Daddy. I can't. It's too hard." Conall pushed and slammed into the invisible wall with as much force as he could muster, and still wasn't able to break through. "Help me."

"This is something you have to do yourself."

"Help me!" Couldn't Daddy see that it was too hard? Conall was only seven. Traveling—pushing through the boundary between the worlds—was beyond him.

"You have to learn, son. You can't stay in one world forever, and I won't always be around to help you."

"But I don't want to. I'm not ready!"

"You are ready. I learned at your age, and so did your grandfather before me. It runs in the family. You can do it. You're strong."

Conall tried again. He took hold of space and time, and pushed and stretched them as far as they would go. For a moment, the fabric of reality bent further than it had before, and he thought this time he might actually poke through. But then it pushed against him once more, casting him back into his exhausted body as it collapsed.

Conall's face turned red. He'd tried a dozen times. Space and time were pliable, yes, but also firm and durable. He could stretch them, but only so far. Tears spilled from his eyes, and he had to work very hard to stop them. He was a failure. He would be the only Doran in fifteen generations to settle on a single world, incapable of pushing the frontier any further. Daddy would be ashamed.

"Conall, don't force it. The harder you push, the harder it pushes back. Remember what I taught you."

"I can't do it."

"You can. The blood of your ancestors is in you. You have their strength."

Conall took a deep breath, shut his eyes, and reached out once more. He seized space and time, grasped them firmly inside his mind, and pushed. The universe met his show of force with one of its own.

Then Daddy's words popped into his head. *Don't force it.* But how could he get through to the other side if he didn't push? This time, he felt around more closely, and examined the weave of the universe in greater detail.

There, a loose thread. How had he missed it before? He pulled, and it slipped free with almost no effort. There was a frightening moment when he could feel the cosmos groan—

where the fibers of reality unraveled, coming apart like a frayed tapestry. Then space and time righted themselves, became whole once again. Where he'd tugged one of those fibers loose, there was now a hole: a soft spot where one world bled into the other.

"Daddy, I did it!"

"Yes," Daddy said, smiling. "You did. I'm proud of you."

"Daddy, can we go through?"

"If you want to." He swept Conall into his arms.

They stepped through together, father and son, and emerged in a new world.

I originally wrote this piece as a Father's Day tribute. If you're a father (especially if you're my father), thank you for loving and encouraging us when we're so young and vulnerable. Whatever great things we do, ultimately rest on the shoulders of our parents.

Alexandria

ALEXANDRIA STOOD BY THE CURB, looking out at the street as the rain poured. Meanwhile, a group of kids played hockey nearby. She didn't ask to join. She knew they'd only laugh.

She stared after them for a moment before making her way along the sidewalk. The clouds above were a roiling sea of gray. The gloom pressed in around her, but it was not an uncomfortable feeling.

She could sense the imagination inside of her, crackling with feral, wild-born magic. The storm amplified her power, so often latent and inactive, and she could feel a whole universe of possibilities fanning out before her.

Alexandria snapped her fingers. A world emerged. She snapped her fingers again. It disappeared.

Let the other kids have their game. She had something better.

Caleb

I was ten the year Caleb disappeared.

We were sitting on his porch, sipping lemonade beneath a pallid morning sun. He was showing me his rock collection, teaching me about all the different kinds of minerals, and how and when and why they were formed.

"The Earth has so many stories to tell," he said with the wisdom of someone much older, and he gazed into a piece of smoky quartz as if it were the solution to some profound primordial puzzle.

He had a way of making the ordinary extraordinary. I didn't know half as much as he did, but it was enough for me to just listen to him talk, to absorb even a fraction of his knowledge.

Then he got quiet, and when I asked what he was thinking he told me he had a secret.

"You have to promise not to tell anyone."

"Okay," I said. "I promise."

He paused. "Dad and I are going away."

"On a trip?"

Caleb shook his head.

"Where? For how long?"

"I don't know. Forever, I guess."

The words formed a fist that punched me in the stomach. I almost doubled over. My best friend was leaving. Tears welled at the corners of my eyes.

"Why do you have to go?"

"I don't know. Dad just said the world's changing, that it's time to move on. He said we're leaving today."

I was shocked. I stared at the street, silent and still, until Caleb spoke again.

"Dad says you can come inside to say goodbye. But you have to promise not to tell anyone."

Caleb opened the door.

I followed.

The inside of his house had always been off-limits. In spite of my pain, I felt a distant thrill. I was doing something that until that day had been forbidden. I expected the interior to be different somehow, like the threshold between Earth and some alien world. But it was only an ordinary living room with a TV, a lamp, and a couch, just like my own house.

"Hello, Daniel," said Caleb's dad, emerging from the hallway with a leather suitcase. He was wearing a black suit and tie, with a matching fedora on his head. "We didn't want to leave without saying goodbye."

"Will you visit?" I asked in desperation.

Caleb glanced up at his dad, who smiled and said, "Maybe. If we can." Then he looked down at my best friend and asked, "Are you ready?"

Eyes downcast, Caleb said he guessed he was.

"Where are you going?" I asked. "Maybe I can write."

But Caleb only shrugged and took his dad's hand. "Bye, Daniel. I'll miss you."

They began to fade.

At first, I didn't understand what I was seeing. I blinked, closed my eyes—I expected it to be some trick of the light. But when I looked at Caleb again, he was transparent, only an apparition in place of the boy he'd once been.

"What's happening?" I thought maybe I was dreaming, that I'd wake up to the familiar relief of my blankets and pillows, secure in the knowledge that Caleb wasn't leaving after all.

"Remember," said Caleb's dad, hardly more than a glimmer, "You have to keep this a secret. We'll visit if we can."

Then they were gone.

I N THE MONTHS that followed, they were the talk of the neighborhood. What had happened to them? Were they okay?

"Caleb was your best friend," Mom said to me once. "Did he tell you anything?"

I shook my head. Yes, Caleb was my best friend and I promised to keep his secret.

Their house is abandoned now. The paint has begun to peel and the yard is a jungle of overgrown weeds. I wander by it from time to time, childhood memories passing through my head like phantoms, wondering if someday he'll return. But deep down, I suspect he's moved on, and I wonder if he would even recognize me if our paths ever crossed again.

Wherever he is, I'm sure he's having an adventure. I only wish I could have joined him.

I based this story off of my own childhood best friend, who moved away when I was ten. Like Caleb, he not only had a passion for rocks and fossils, but he left an indelible mark on my soul that I'll carry with me forever. This piece and the memories it stirred touched me so much that I ended up writing a related novel with the same title.

The Foolish Apprentice

"I TOLD YOU how to do this already."

"Yes, sir," said Jess, stumbling over the title, tiny beads of sweat dotting his forehead. "Sorry. I forgot."

Amos sighed. Hovering over his apprentice, he watched with consternation as he made all the wrong weaves, missteps he'd tried to correct more than a dozen times during the past week.

Suddenly there was a bright electric flash like a strobe, and Jess staggered back.

"Jess!" cried Amos, though he was too late to stop it. He was equal parts relieved and enraged to find he'd come away from his mistake uninjured. "Goddammit, Jess! You could've killed us both."

Jess looked back at him blankly.

"Here," said Amos, collecting himself. He raised his hands into the air. "I'll show you again."

He proceeded to step through basic fingerings he'd learned when he was ten. He penetrated empty space, took hold of two threads. He tucked one behind the other and twisted until the pair was taut. Then he relaxed his grip and let the weave unravel slowly between his fingers. It emitted a soft, golden glow.

"The weave for light," said Amos flatly. "The tighter the twist, the more energy that's released, the brighter the light."

"I mostly had it," said Jess, rising to his own defense. His cheeks had turned pink. "I just gave it too much tension."

"And almost blinded us both." Amos snarled. "You can't just let go of a weave like that. You have to let it unwind slowly, keep it under control. Magicians have burned themselves to cinders for making mistakes like that."

Jess balled his hands into fists.

This wasn't working. Simon had said the boy was headstrong, and that was true enough, but what he'd left out was that the boy was also a fool. Take either attribute apart from the other and you'd have something Amos could work with. If the boy were headstrong but talented, he could find some way to channel his pride toward a healthy confidence. If the boy were foolish but humble, he could be patient, step through the basics over and over again, confident that he would pay attention and eventually learn. But a headstrong fool? There was nothing to be done for that.

"Listen," said Amos, and he had to swallow a vile insult that had risen up into his throat. "I know you're anxious to get through the basics—that you want to be a great magician like your father—but you're young. You know nothing, and it takes time. Your father was a great man because he knew when to listen as well as when to lead, because he spent hours in his workshop after you kids had gone to bed and drilled himself in the essentials."

"My father?" shouted Jess, leaping to his feet. "What do you know about my father?"

"Quite a bit more than you, apparently," said Amos, trying to keep his voice level. "He never would have put up with your refusal to listen, your stubbornness in the face of correction. I would've thought you'd know better."

"My father said I was destined for greatness," argued Jess.

"Maybe. If you'd spent more time under his tutelage before he died, perhaps you would've learned what it takes to be great. But now? I'm beginning to think you'll never learn."

Jess looked like he was going to say something. Tight cords bulged from his neck. But after a moment the rage drained out of him and his head fell into his hands.

"He always made it look so easy," said Jess in a vulnerable tone that Amos had not heard before. "Before he died, he made it look so easy, and then Simon tried to teach me, and I couldn't get it, and I felt so stupid. I got frustrated, and I thought, *if only Dad were still here to teach me himself.*"

A tear fell from one of the boy's eyes, and Amos's appraisal of him changed. Perhaps Jess could be reached after all. Maybe his pride was a façade—a front he'd erected to protect a battered ego further embittered by the premature loss of his father. With some patience and kindness (God knew this was not his forte), perhaps the boy would turn out all right.

"Jess," said Amos, "your father spoke very highly of you. I believe you can do this, but you have to be open to correction. You can't take it as a personal affront every time I point out that you're doing something wrong. Part of your father's greatness was his willingness to own up to mistakes and fix them. If you do the same, you can be like him, I'm sure of it."

"You think so?" Jess looked up then, and Amos's heart softened.

"I know so." He placed an affectionate hand on the boy's shoulder. He would take him under his wing, he decided, not just as a mentor, but as a guardian and a friend.

Jess nodded, sniffled, and reached toward his nose to wipe away more tears. "Show me once more?"

Amos reached into empty space again, and this time Jess paid attention.

The Puddle

I REMEMBER STANDING on the playground at school after a storm, my hands numb from the cold, my nostrils filled with the scent of wet earth and asphalt. I peered down at the blacktop, made slick and shiny by the rain, and I scurried to where the water had pooled into a large sprawling puddle. I stared, transfixed by that shallow body that seemed so deep, and my breath caught. Was that just a reflection I could see, or was it, perhaps, some exceedingly rare glimpse of another world?

I felt that all I had to do was jump, and I would find myself falling, tumbling, down and down into endless blue. Or perhaps floating, flying, borne by great billowing clouds and fearsome bellowing winds, up into that vast ocean of upside-down sky. Holding my breath, I took a leap of faith and jumped. But beneath my feet to break my fall were the shoes of an upside down boy.

He looked just like me. I gazed down, sad, and he looked back up with the same doleful expression.

I stepped back, and the boy beneath my feet did the same. I waited, hoping he would go away, but when I slowly craned my neck forward to make sure my path was clear, I saw the boy had returned. I took a deep breath. If only I could slip past him. If only I could trick him into moving away. I cast another furtive glance over the edge of the puddle, but the boy was still there.

I made as if to draw away, then suddenly whirled and lunged into the air with eyes closed. I felt the rush of frigid morning wind as it whooshed and whipped over my arms and shoulders. I was certain I'd outsmarted him.

The puddle shattered as my feet struck the water, and a magnificent spray of shimmering liquid glass rained down around me. For a fraction of a second, I was certain my body would clear that thin barrier between the worlds, tumbling and falling into infinity. When my descent was stopped short, I opened my eyes. I looked down, and there was the boy, gazing up at me. His face was set in a solemn expression. There would be no freedom that day.

I stood and stared at the boy who had denied me access to his endless world of blue. Only after the bell rang and a teacher took me by the shoulder did I go, and as I proceeded toward the dim and dreary classroom where I would be locked away for the remainder of the day, I glanced back at the puddle, that gateway into another world. The boy was gone, but it was too late.

A captive sun pushed through charcoal clouds, and, throughout the day, while I bent lower over a desk with my head in my hands, it drank up all the water. That temporary portal into another existence receded, falling into itself until at last there was hardly more than a drop. All the while, I imagined the mist that would have risen up around it, the soul of a dying world.

After school, I stood over where the puddle had once been. I mourned the loss of a world. I mourned the loss of freedom.

When I was a boy, I would pretend the reflections I saw in puddles were temporary gateways into other worlds. This story is about that fantasy, which I've never completely stopped believing.

The Stone

"**P**SST, BOY."

Adrian glanced at the alley, where an old man hunched against a brick wall.

"Boy," he repeated. "Come here. I have something for you."

Curious and heedless of potential danger, Adrian did as he was told. When he was close enough to get a good look at the man's soiled rags, and to smell that he hadn't bathed in weeks, the man glanced sideways, as if nervous he was being watched.

"Take this."

Adrian looked down at the man's closed fist.

"A gift," he said, shoving a smooth round object into Adrian's left hand. A moment later, he darted off into the shadows.

Adrian examined his prize.

A stone.

Brow furrowed, he continued home and placed it atop a shelf. He didn't think about it anymore that day.

Meanwhile, the stone waited.

That night, when Adrian returned to his room to sleep, he found the stone where he'd left it. He picked it up and carried it with him to bed. Beneath the moonlight that spilled through the window, it almost seemed to glow. Suddenly, his imagination went wild, and he was certain this simple object could reveal the universe's deepest secrets.

When exhaustion overtook him and he finally fell asleep, the stone was still clutched between his fingers.

He dreamed that night.

He was tumbling between the stars, falling, flying with jets like cosmic sparks shooting through space. Galaxies spiraled in the distance; galaxies of every shape and size, whirling, colliding, bursting in coruscating flashes.

Adrian felt lost, but he was not afraid because he held the stone.

"The cosmos is yours now," said the voice of the man he'd met in the alley. The universe shook with the force of his words. They were a binding, the oldest and most powerful kind.

And then he was opening his eyes, and all he could see or hear was the pale light of the moon and the chirping of crickets outside. He glanced at the ordinary-looking stone, still firmly grasped in his left hand. It felt warm.

Adrian smiled.

Wish

" **S** EE YOU LATER, Shit Face," said Steve, spitting on the ground. Lucas, crouched on the sidewalk where the bully had pushed him down, glanced up and tried very hard not to cry. Steve signaled to his lackeys that it was time to go.

A couple of minutes later, Lucas scrambled to his feet, wiped the dust and dirt from his jeans, and continued walking.

Steve had cornered him on his way home from school again. Lucas hated the condescending smile, the insults, the shoves and headlocks and kicks. The kid was a monster, and Lucas wished he were dead.

He passed the school yard, glancing cautiously over his shoulder in case Steve decided to come back, and brooded with his gaze lowered to the sidewalk.

That was how he noticed the match.

The dingy, partially consumed matchbox lay open in the gutter, a single unused match peeking out from the packaging.

It's a well-known fact that there's nothing so attractive to a nine-year-old boy as an unused match, and all thoughts of Steve and his minions vanished as he knelt to retrieve the forbidden object.

He looked over his shoulder again, this time to make sure there were no grown-ups to see what he was doing. Then he picked it up and turned it over to examine the cover.

Fritz Gentlemen's Club, where all your dreams come true.

Lucas didn't know what a gentleman's club was, but he knew all about wishes. He tore the remaining match from its cardboard binding and held it up to the light.

"I wish I had more," he said with a sigh before striking. The tip erupted in a bright green flame.

Lucas goggled. He'd never seen fire like this before. The flame crept dangerously close to his fingers, and the sharp bite of instant heat made him drop the match.

"Ow!" he cried, pulling his fingers into his mouth.

He looked down again at the matchbook…and beheld ten unused matches.

"No way."

The match had granted his wish. Lucas thought of Steve, and his mind ignited with possibilities.

Decisions

Introduction

Decisions have consequences. Sometimes, the consequences are insignificant and we can charge headlong into the unknown without a care for where we might end up. Other times, the consequences are serious, even catastrophic, and we find ourselves paralyzed by indecision.

Whether our choices are moral, logistic, or convenient in nature, they always represent a crossroads in our life, a point along the journey where we must choose from two or more possibilities that will carry us off to altogether different places: some marvelous, others perilous.

At times, we may be tempted to press the pause button. But as dangerous as our choices might be, we cannot stand still, for what is choosing to remain stationary but a decision made by default? All we can do, then, is examine our hearts, and after due deliberation take the next step into the unknown, praying the entire way that we won't be led astray.

Choices

JANELLE STOOD BEFORE a network of interconnected roads, celestial paths across space and time that fanned out into the horizon and beyond, forking and dividing in an increasingly complex and unforeseeable set of possible futures. So many choices. It was dizzying for her, thinking of all the places she might go, all the things she might see. Some were good. Others were not.

She hesitated.

She'd spent her whole life preparing for this moment, taught by her tribe from birth that someday she would have to stand before the Great Road and walk toward her destiny.

They'd promised her a guide, someone who would travel beside her unseen and pick her up when she couldn't go on by herself. But now, at the outset of her journey, she felt alone, and that made her afraid.

Faced with an infinite array of choices, how was she supposed to pick the right one? She could see one, perhaps two steps ahead; she could calculate the probabilities and possible outcomes as she saw them, but beyond? Her journey might have promising beginnings, yet end in disaster only a few steps in. Each step forward, each fork in the road was another risk, and one way or the other, whether her travels were long or short, fortunate or unfortunate, no path continued forever. One day, at the end of her road, there would be a door, ready to open to the other side. Not knowing where that door might be or where it would lead terrified her.

But she couldn't stand here forever. Some had spent their entire lives paralyzed by indecision, too afraid to move. They had eventually been escorted away in shame, forced through their own door before their journeys had even begun. Janelle had no desire to miss her journey.

The end, she realized, would come for her whether she was ready or not, so what was the point in stalling? She would have to go, hope she was headed in the right direction and trust that her unseen guide would catch her if she fell. Her tribe had said the first step would be the hardest, and that once she got moving she wouldn't want to stop. It was time to see if that was true.

She took a deep breath, her heart thumping in her chest like an overworked piston. She glanced down at her feet, swallowed a lump that had formed in the back of her throat. She lifted one foot, then the other.

There was a shift, an instant of double vision as the world changed, and then her surroundings resolved. She looked around, overcome by cosmic beauty such as she had never seen before. She was overcome with joy. Now she was hooked. The fear remained, but was superseded by a deeper desire, an inborn need to discover what else was out there. There was a whole road just for her. There would be joys and sorrows, conveniences and hardships, but in the end, it would all add up to one hell of an adventure.

Janelle found the next fork. She stepped. The world shifted.

Doing the Right Thing

Max looked down at his feet. Gazed back up at the desolate street. Watched as his breath plumed before him like dragon's breath in the cold midnight air.

He waited.

How had he gotten to this point? He took hold of who he was, and, like a string, he tried to follow it back through time. But that string was so tangled and twisted that he found he wasn't able to follow it very far.

His father had introduced him to this lifestyle when he was a child, but that was no excuse. He'd had plenty of opportunities to escape. So why hadn't he run off when he'd had the chance?

A shadow caught his eye, and he turned in its direction just in time for the darkness before him to melt, morph, coalesce into the figure of another man. The figure dropped a cigarette to the ground, tamped it beneath the heel of a black leather boot, and tipped a broad fedora in Max's direction.

"Evening," said the man, and oddly Max was reminded of John Wayne. He reached out with a thick muscular hand. Max grasped it in a cautious handshake.

"Evening," echoed Max. Butterflies churned in his stomach. This was it. This was when it would all go to Hell.

"The boss has another job for you," said the man, reaching in his pocket for a second cigarette. "A gentleman by the name of Richardson. Says he'll pay quite a sum if you can do this one right." A stainless steel lighter sparked, ignited. The man lit up and took a long drag. "Sounds important."

Max shifted his feet and shivered as the frigid air pressed in around him.

Richardson. Max wondered how he'd crossed the boss's path, and he could only speculate on how terribly he'd fucked up to warrant the boss's intervention.

Max would be asked to introduce himself, to befriend him, to gain his trust so that he could ultimately lure him to his demise. It was a skill he was good at, a skill that ran in his family: the ability to read minds, to get at the heart of a person's needs and desires. That, along with a pinch of charisma, won them over every time.

No doubt Richardson would be dethroned. That was the boss's term. It meant he would be stripped of everything but his life, imprisoned just outside the range of human perception, forced to look on in despair from the shadows as someone else stole his identity, his life, and enjoyed all the things that were rightfully his. He would be doomed to wander the Earth in exile forever.

Like a disinherited prince, the boss was wont to say, hence the term "dethroned."

But Max wanted no part of it, not anymore. He'd ruined too many lives, had betrayed too many people's trust, consigning them to fates worse than death. He'd foolishly followed in his father's footsteps, but he would follow no further.

"Actually," said Max in a strangely quiet voice, "I wanted to talk to you about that."

The man squinted. "Yeah?"

"Well, I—" What was he doing? The boss would tear him apart. Perhaps he, too, would be dethroned. It would be a fitting punishment, atonement for his own crimes.

"Go on," said the man.

"I mean, it's just that— I thought maybe I'd go to school, try to make a different kind of life for myself."

The man stared at Max, boring a hole through his skull. Then, without warning, he threw back his head and laughed, a hearty mirth that took Max aback.

"School? You're a funny guy, Max. A very funny guy."

"I'm serious. I—"

"Stop," said the man, and just like that the laughter was gone. "You'll want to stop joking, because sometimes," said the man, backing Max into a brick wall, "jokes have consequences."

Max swallowed. He'd prepared for this moment. He'd practiced what he would say in front of a mirror for hours. But now that he was here and actually saying it, the imagined bluster and bravado had evaporated.

"I...I can't," Max stammered. "Not anymore. It's too much."

"The boss gave you everything. And your father. And your grandfather."

"I appreciate everything the boss—"

"Bullshit," said the man, poking him hard in the chest, "I don't think you do. The boss needs you, Max. Your family has a rare skill that he needs, and, in return, there's nothing he wouldn't do for you. And now you're going to deny him. Why, because it's hard? Because it hurts? Because suddenly your conscience bothers you and you want to sleep better at night?"

"This is wrong," said Max, slowly picking up steam. He'd already pushed too far; his fate had been sealed the moment he opened his mouth. "You know it is. I can't undo what my family's done, but I don't have to be a part of it anymore."

The man glared at him, goggling as if Max had just proclaimed with religious zeal that the Earth was flat. Finally, after a long silence, he spoke. "So, that's it then?"

"Yes," said Max, and he shrugged. "I have to do the right thing."

"All right." The man released Max, and he slid down onto the sidewalk, his legs suddenly too weak to support his weight. "You'll be hearing from the boss soon." The man stepped back, melted once more into the shadows. "Real soon."

Once again, Max waited.

Sacrifice

Arnold stood in the middle of a darkened desert beside a man whose name he did not know.

"I didn't ask for this," said Arnold.

"No," the man agreed. "You didn't."

He sighed and gazed up at the stars, knowing it would be the last time he saw them.

He'd been given a choice: lose the world for himself and save it for others, or stay and fail to prevent the world's end. There were no compromises, no half measures.

The man shrugged his shoulders. "You could just walk away, you know."

"No," said Arnold after a long pause. "I can't."

The man offered him a sad smile. "That's why I picked you."

Arnold took one final drag of air from an atmosphere that no longer belonged to him. Then he took the man's hand, and together they disappeared into the dark.

Depression

Introduction

I suffered for much of my young adult life with depression. It was a terrible debilitating monster that sometimes kept me in bed for hours during the day, that held my writing back for years and almost stopped me from publishing, that in every way you can think of, made my life dark, dreary, and miserable, all the while convincing me that the problems in my head were my fault. A season of therapy combined with determination and a lot of hard work got me through the worst of it, but to this day, I still from time to time spot depression's dark shadow, creeping up from behind, waiting for the perfect moment to strike again, and I remember I must remain vigilant, lest it consume me and pull me back into the darkness once more.

The stories in this category are all, in some way or another, attempts to describe the horrors of depression and the devastating effects they can have on a person when left untreated.

Half-Life

FINGERS REACHING, CREEPING, curling around my neck like choking vines. Draining my life. I struggle, try to pry them off my vulnerable skin.

It taunts me, utters its low, susurrus laugh like dried leaves—like rattlesnake's skin as it slithers across dry desert sand.

I always manage to survive, in spite of its debilitating grip, but only just. Mine is a sort of half-life, forever suspended between the dark and the light. And beneath me, the creature in the shadows beckons me to give up, to let go, to allow myself to fall into its insatiable jaws.

It knows I weaken, that I have not the strength to escape and fly toward the light. It does not age, but instead bides its time, for it knows I can only go on for so long before I falter.

How long can I live without rescue before my grip loosens? How long can I survive?

Nightmare

Sleep. It weighs her down, muddles her thoughts. She can't let it drag her under. If she falls asleep now, she'll die.

She can feel the creature salivating in the shadows, waiting for her to tumble into its toothy maw. It's hungry and wants to feed.

Sleep. It sings of peace, promises solace and renewal even as it threatens obliteration. The world tilts as she turns her head. She can sense the creature in every corner, hiding just beyond the range of her perception, an ambassador from the underworld who will steal her life the moment she departs from the waking world.

But her eyes are heavy. So heavy. Like tiny lead curtains closing at the final act of her life.

Consciousness gutters like a dying flame.

She can hear its voice.

You are mine.

Yes, she thinks, too drowsy to resist. *I am yours.* And she finds herself drifting toward the dark, drifting toward death, heedless of the annihilation that awaits.

Come to me.

She closes her eyes.

You are mine.

A cold embrace. Then darkness.

Nothing Lasts Forever

I THOUGHT IT would last forever. I thought I could do no wrong, that no matter what I did, it would always be with me. Then it up and went and I never saw it again.

I cry every night, pausing only to dab at red and swollen eyelids. I drop to my knees and pray. I beg the creator of the cosmos to bring it back. I promise not to take it for granted, to give it the veneration it deserves. But my prayers always go unanswered.

I am only a shell of my former self, a hollowed-out husk who's lived for centuries in seclusion, too afraid and too ashamed to dwell among others.

The only time I speak is when I emerge naked from beneath my ancient stone bridge in the middle of the night to call out into the darkness, to speak its name, hoping it will hear my call. Hours pass before I go back inside, cold and damp, and only when I fall asleep does it come back to haunt me in my dreams.

The Walking Dead

THE MAGIC IS GONE.

I'm not sure when I noticed. It didn't go all at once. It lingered, even as it slowly leached away, until the universe had been sucked dry, a desiccated husk.

I wander a broken world denuded, a disinherited prince. There are no sorrows, no joys; just a dull, flat, aching despair, my soul's pleading cry, a desire to live once again. But the spark is gone now; there is no life within me.

I am the walking dead.

Abandonment

Introduction

From first grade all the way to my senior year in high school, I was bullied. I was taunted, kicked, and humiliated. Like a circus sideshow, I was put on display for the amusement of my adolescent peers. I made friends early on, only for many to abandon me later as a sacrifice before the mystical altar of popularity.

I won't pretend that I know what it feels like to be abandoned in more serious ways, like a child with a deadbeat mother or father, or a spouse whose partner left them without a word in the middle of the night, never to be heard from again. As bad as elementary school and high school were, I was blessed to have a strong family, with parents who loved me and gave me all the support in the world, and I continue to be blessed with a wife who understands and loves me unconditionally. I will say, however, with the utmost confidence that being abandoned by your peers during your most vulnerable years may be crippling; it leaves a mark, an ugly festering sore that never completely heals. It's something you carry into adulthood, whether you want to or not, and it's likely to color your perceptions, making it difficult to trust, or to love.

It is for this reason that I have a profound sensitivity toward those who've been bullied or abandoned, and why I often find myself writing about such struggles.

Better Off Inside

L IGHT PENETRATES MY EYES. For a moment, I gaze up, squint through the bars of a prison abandoned for centuries, and consider my escape. Then the light begins to burn and I look away.

The bars have rusted through, have even crumbled to powder in places. Yet I remain.

All of us remain.

Part of the prison's success was the way the guards got into our heads, the way they convinced us we deserved persecution—that we were better off inside.

The world is dangerous for a monster like you. We locked you away for your own good.

Humanity ultimately forgot us, as humanity forgets so many things. They were free; we were not. Out of sight, out of mind. I imagine our existence became the subject of legend, and that, once enough time had passed, even the legend began to fade. I don't remember how long we've been down here, nor do I remember when they stopped sending their guards. I only know they don't hold power over us any longer.

But we won't leave, because fear has become our new jailer.

Don't you think I yearn to be free? Don't you think I would give my soul to break out of this cage that binds me beneath the earth, to crawl through the shaft that connects us to the surface and enjoy fresh sunshine once again?

Ask any of us and we'll tell you the same thing: We fear what will happen if we leave, what you'll do to us if we're discovered again.

You enjoy your light above. We'll make the darkness our own.

Can You See Me?

Can you see me? I'm standing right in front of you.

I'm the guy with the soiled, unkempt beard; the haunted eyes; the mouth that hangs slightly agape in an expression of permanent disbelief. I don't bother trying to get your attention. I know you'll just look past me—that you'll either be unable or unwilling to acknowledge me for who and what I am.

The world, once hospitable to my kind, has shunned me. I was cast into the streets like a dog banished from its pack, left to forage for myself in the dim shadow of the forgotten.

I cannot die, not unless the world dies with me. Oh, how I wait with bitter anticipation, how I labor for that day.

There are advantages to a life unseen.

Grace

G RACE CLUTCHES A RAGGED teddy bear to her chest. It reminds her of her parents. The memories are bittersweet.

She gazes up, squints when her eyes reach the bright lines of yellow light that penetrate between the wooden slats a hundred feet above. She blinks away tears.

She sidles to the right, her long dress brushing the dirt beneath her legs, and she feels the tug of iron chains binding her to the stone wall. She expects it, though it continues to fill her with despair. She returns to her previous position and the chains slacken. She closes her eyes and dozes.

She never meant them harm. She came after her parents died and left her orphaned in the woods outside their village. They took her in, fed her, clothed her. They took her to church. Taught her to pray. Then they discovered she was different.

They called her a demon. Spat on her. Beat her. Dug a prison beneath the earth, clapped her in chains and left her there to rot.

For the first few days, she'd cried out in disbelief. Trembling and wailing, she begged them between sobs to take her back. She promised to be good, but nobody listened. She was an uncomfortable truth that was better off buried and forgotten.

She heard their whispers, knew they expected her to die. Yet years passed without food or water and she survived. They said it was unnatural, that she was the spawn of Satan. Every now and then, one of them would gaze down between the wooden slats, peer into her tear-streaked eyes and look away.

A generation passed. The children grew up and ventured out in search of better lives, and one by one the remaining inhabitants grew old and died. The last of them to peer down into her prison had white, wispy hair and a thin gray beard. He cocked his head at her, hesitated, and moved closer, as if wondering what to do. Then he gritted his teeth, clutched his chest, closed his eyes, and collapsed.

The first years of her life had been filled with love and light. She'd danced beneath the trees, sustained by the sun, the wind, the earth, and the sky, a child of wild, nature-born magic. But bound beneath the earth in isolation, her good nature soured. Her heart grew hard, and spite consumed her until her only wish was to set the world on fire, and to look on with delight as the skin of those who imprisoned her crackled, blistered, and popped.

She knows that one day she'll be free. Perhaps her chains will rust through completely and she'll dig herself out. Or perhaps someone will wander by unknowing and rescue her.

It's only a matter of time.

Grace dons a wicked smile.

The villagers could have bred a saint. Instead, they bred a monster.

The Stranger

I SLAM MY FISTS against the wall, and you stare at me until I divert my gaze. Then you look away and give me a wide berth, backing off to a safe distance. Desperate for help, I cry out to you, and that's when you scurry around a corner and disappear from sight. I gaze at the sky and loose a hailstorm of curses.

All around me, glittering crystal towers reach for the heavens alongside metal trees with lights that hang over roads where self-propelled vehicles rocket toward foreign destinations. I've never seen such opulence, not in all the centuries of my royal upbringing.

Above me is a sign in a language I don't understand. I try in vain to decipher the unfamiliar script.

GOVERNOR GEORGE DEUKMEJIAN COURTHOUSE
SUPERIOR COURT OF CALIFORNIA
COUNTY OF LOS ANGELES

I shake my head, as if doing so will dispel the alien environment like a bad dream.

Banished. The word echoes through the chaotic corridors of my mind. Banished for a crime I didn't commit, stripped of my title, my citizenship, my world.

They broke into the palace while I slept, and threw me into a moldering dungeon. From there, I was brought before a tribunal, and, despite my vehement denials, I was convicted and sentenced to exile.

They dragged me to a towering rock-face etched with symbols only the priests could understand, flickering torches in iron sconces casting a dim illumination. The priests produced a guttural chant, and light exploded from the wall, no longer smooth stone, but one that revealed a passageway to someplace else.

In the presence of the assembly, I proclaimed my innocence one last time. They spit in my face, made obscene gestures, and shoved me through. Fire consumed my body, rending skin and flesh, until I passed out.

I woke here, in front of this building where I've remained ever since. My robes, now dingy and threadbare; my hair, tangled and feral.

I know what you thought when you saw me pounding the wall, crying out in words that would have sounded to you like inarticulate war cries. He's crazy. Once, in my own world, I would have thought the same.

I stare at the wall again, seeing not the stone that stands before me, but the world beyond. I may not be crazy yet, but I will be before long.

Cosmic Matters

Introduction

This introduction is hard for me to write, in part because it touches on vulnerable aspects of my soul that I usually hide away, and in part because it's not something I entirely understand myself.

I am a man on a quest. Like Stephen King's Roland quests for the Dark Tower, I quest for Truth with a capital T. I have absolute faith that it exists. I also have absolute faith that I have no idea what it is or how to go about finding it. I only know I have to keep searching, and that I can't give up. If I stop—if I die without at least making the effort—my soul will die with me. I've been on this quest for a few years now. How exactly it started or why, I can only offer three fragmentary insights.

The first: I've always had a deep love for science, and have always wanted to know what the universe is and how it works. While many kids in my class were talking about popular movies and TV shows, I was asking questions about atoms and molecules, about the nature of the Earth and the solar system, the stars and all the things that lie beyond. At one point in my life, I pursued a major in physics and math, and only backed off because circumstances wouldn't allow me to go further.

The second: I was raised nominally Christian, and eventually became a Christian of the Catholic variety in high school. For a time, I was deeply religious, and I remained that way until college, when I started to question everything, as young adults are generally wont to do.

The third: Serious doubts about my faith, along with serious doubts about my ability to know anything at all, combined with the fact that I was suffering through social anxiety, depression, and other distresses made for an intensely uncomfortable period of my life that spanned a great many years. Today, I'm stuck in a weird sort of limbo where I practice a faith I don't quite believe, because a part of me (whether reason, fear, or both, I honestly don't know) feels that it might be true, while another part of me is convinced the truth lies elsewhere. Like a caterpillar trapped in its cocoon, I'm suspended between contradictory states and have no idea who or what I'm going to be when the process is complete and I emerge on the other side of time.

All of this combines to form within me the kind of heart in which science, philosophy, and religion fascinate me—and haunt me. Science gives me a burning desire to know what the universe *is*, while philosophy and religion impel me to discover *why*.

This is why, on my blog (and in this book), you'll see me explore creation myths, the notion of life beyond our four experienced dimensions of space-time, and the concept of the afterlife. It's my futile grasping at straws, my imagination reaching out to fill in the pieces that reason alone has so far failed to explain.

Lady of the Stars

THE LADY OF THE STARS found her when she was only an infant, an orphaned ball of molten rock hurtling through the cosmos. She adopted her. Nursed her. Nurtured her. She named her Earth. And in the eons that followed, she thrived.

Mountains sprang forth from her surface like newly germinated flowers. Water condensed, pooled, bulged into vast sprawling oceans.

And then perhaps Earth's most important accomplishment: life. First were born the amino acids. Then the single-celled organisms. Then the plants and animals. Each form was more complex than the last, and each was assembled under the expectant gaze of the Lady of the Stars.

Soon the planet teemed with life. And finally, Earth's crowning achievement: humanity.

Humans. Her daughter's children. The Lady swelled with pride. She loved them as her own, spoiled them with all they could ask for and more.

There was peace.

But the Lady had sisters, and they were jealous, for they were barren and could have no children of their own.

"I'm like you," she protested when they confronted her. "Earth was not my own. I adopted her. Can you not scour the cosmos for your own adoptive children?"

But they were too consumed by their hatred to hear her words. Instead, they bound her, cast her outside the boundaries of space and time.

Earth became distressed, torn by the competing interests of the Lady's sisters. Humans mirrored their divisions and formed factions of their own. There were wars. People died. Earth rumbled in pain.

The Lady, hearing her daughter's distant cries, was overcome by grief. She broke the chains that bound her, and today she runs toward her child, toward her grandchildren.

Will she come too late?

Planter of Worlds

ANDI REACHES INTO a faded leather pouch and produces a handful of seeds. She scatters them about the ground. Waters them. Moves on.

She waits for them to grow.

She is a Sower, a planter of worlds. She wanders the cosmos, the last of her kind, spreading her celestial seed. Wherever she goes, worlds spring up in her wake, quivering with wild, newborn magic.

Long ago, her people filled the fertile fields of the universe, sowing and nurturing celestial objects of every kind. Stars burst to life in the darkness of empty space and bore an abundance of planetary fruit. It was their greatest work, their crowning glory.

But when they were finished, they moved on. The canvas had been filled, they said, and they were ready to plant bigger, better gardens. But Andi couldn't let it go. She saw that it was beautiful, but also imperfect, and she knew that with time she could make it better.

So Andi picked up her seed pouch and got to work, planting a world here, a star there. Each sowing brought the cosmos that much closer to perfection.

Andi knows her work will never be complete, and that perfection is an eternal struggle, something to be aimed for but never reached. She understands something the rest of her kind did not: A labor of love is never finished; it must be tended to assiduously.

She hopes that one day they'll return. Perhaps if they lay eyes upon her work, they'll stay to help.

Roots

THE UNIVERSE WAS WEAKENING.

Betty could feel it fraying around the edges, the evil beyond pounding against the celestial gates. The cosmos wouldn't hold for long, and when its defenses fell, it wouldn't just be this universe that would suffer. Hers was the cornerstone, the center of all existence, the universe in which all others derived their being. If she didn't do something soon, all would be lost.

She closed her eyes. Took a deep breath. Let her soul slip from her body. The cosmos absorbed her into itself, until she was sailing across space and time. The fabric of existence quaked and shuddered with the force of the Darkness's attacks, and she felt herself falter, guttering like a flame caught in a strong wind. But she would not let the world she loved die with her.

She pressed on.

She let the Darkness draw her, let it tug her along the macrocosm's star-spangled surface like a lure. It was hungry, eager to consume, and she would use its hunger against it.

One rumbling quake after another, each like a mountain hurled at her from a world-sized slingshot. Soon enough, she found herself at the source, a bulge in the cosmic substrate, a festering pustule that was growing like cancer just beneath the surface.

I can't do this. The thought skittered along the membrane of her mind, but she ignored it. She could, and she would. All of reality depended on it.

She let the Darkness pull her in further, until the g-forces from that supernatural black hole threatened to pull her apart. Then she reached out—it was like sticking the arms of her body in tar—took hold, and slowly peeled back the layers of empty space.

The Darkness shuddered, reeled.

WHAT IS THIS?

It was aware of what she was doing now. She had to work quickly. She inserted herself into the place between, felt for the roots of this deadly celestial blight, and pulled.

Another rumbling shudder.

I WILL CONSUME YOU.

Waves of despair crashed over her, and she faltered. She could feel those poor souls who were trapped on the other side, wailing in eternal despair. Like a hook, dark emotions began to reel her in.

But Betty wasn't having any of that. She sent out roots of her own, a blinding sprawl of interconnected fibers. They anchored her to space and time, where she stood fast, and let the Darkness's greedy tugging work against itself.

Sure enough, the more ardently it struggled to pull her in, the more the hold of its own roots weakened, unable to withstand the intense shearing forces.

There was one final shudder, one that nearly did her in, and then Betty felt the first root snap. One by one, the others followed.

WHAT HAVE YOU DONE? the Darkness bellowed, its disbelieving howl rippling across the universe. *I AM UNDONE.*

The last of its roots disengaged and the Darkness was cast out at last, hurtling into the void beyond.

Exhausted, Betty surveyed the damage. It was extensive, she thought, but with time and help it would heal. She considered her body back home, an unfathomable number of miles and eons behind her, and let it go. She was part of the universe now, ageless and eternal.

She extended her roots as far as they would go, hooked into the wounded patch of space and time like a scab. Yes, she thought again. The cosmos would heal. She knew that together they would grow into something stronger, something greater.

The Darkness would return, but with her and the cosmos joined, they would be ready.

Way Station

Come. Sit. Warm yourself by my fire. It's not every day someone makes it out this far. You must have many questions.

What's that? You'll have to come closer. My ears aren't what they used to be. Yes, that's what I thought you asked. You're not going to make this easy on an old man, are you?

Very well. Stop looking at me like that. I'll tell you what you want to know. It was a long time ago, you understand, and I can't be expected to remember everything. These were the old times, when the world was still new, still blazing with the wild, newborn magic of creation.

Yes, as a matter of fact I was there when the world was made, and I'm old enough to remember what came before it, too. But we can talk about that later.

Now, where was I? The creation of the world. I was there when the Maker spoke the Word. There were many words that came after, of course, but this was the first. This was the prototype, the foundation on which everything else was built, the fount from which all other words derive their meanings and their power. It was the Word that gave birth to the world, the Word that nourished the world, the Word that even now sustains the world.

Well now, what else would the universe be made of? At the root of everything, at the heart of creation, there is only will made manifest. Quite simply, the world exists because the Maker wishes it, and it's a good thing for you and I, wouldn't you agree?

You say your father told you a different story? I see. He said the universe started with a bang, that the world we know today was birthed not by the utterance of a divine Word, but within the celestial light of a star? Well, he's not wrong, you know.

I was there, I should know. As an Elder, I witnessed it all. The fireworks were rather spectacular. A shame you couldn't have been there.

What do you mean, you demand the truth? You believe I've deceived you, that both stories can't be true? That's the trouble with you humans. You're so quick to dismiss a mystery as paradox and contradiction.

Yes, it was the Word that created the world, just as it was the motion of matter and energy that produced the world. One was the cause, the other the method.

And I'll tell you a secret: The world isn't finished yet. That's right. How can it be, when everything is in a constant state of change?

I'll tell you another secret: You're a part of it. The Word is within you, as it is within me, and by the simple act of living, by making decisions and effecting change, you become a not so insignificant part of the Maker's work. The mark you leave on the world is indelible and everlasting.

You don't understand? Well, I'll tell you one more secret: Neither do I. What is life, after all, but one grand, cosmic mystery? If you didn't leave the light of my fire with more questions than answers, I'd question your intelligence. But I knew you were special from the start. That's why you made it this far, and now I'm here to teach you that life's a journey, that my humble fire is but a way station, one among many.

No, please. Stay as long as you like. Some move on quickly, but others linger, and there's no shame in that. Take all the time you need to ask, ponder, and learn. No two journeys are ever the same, and some require more deliberation than others.

Just be warned: There is no going back, no returning to the way things were. You should have learned that already, having made it this far, but I want to be certain you understand that time and change are a one-way trip.

One day, the Word will return to the Maker, and you and I and everything else will be swept away along with it. That is the ultimate destination, the point at which all journeys converge. There can be no turning back, and you would do well to look forward and to keep your eyes fixed on the horizon.

Yes, it is a mystery, one of many, and unfortunately, there are no satisfying answers, at least on this side of time.

No, I think that's enough for now. Rest. The stars along with my fire will keep you warm, and when you wake, I'll be here to answer more of your questions.

That's why I'm here, after all.

Death and the Afterlife

Introduction

Death. It is the end of everything we know. Is it a shunting of the soul into light or oblivion? Read my introduction to the "Cosmic Matters" category, and you'll learn why the concepts of death and the afterlife hold so much power over me.

Death was never something I thought about when I was younger. Even when I went to mass and was taught what the Church believes about the fate of the soul after passing, it was only a theoretical complication, a troubling idea that lay somewhere in a distant land. But now, as I find myself growing older, as I begin to tire more easily, as I slowly lose the enthusiasm and energy I once possessed, the concept of death begins to come into view just on the edge of the horizon. Though I'm still young, and it's far off yet (I hope, God willing), I feel my mortality creeping up on me, and I know it will catch up before too long, crooking a finger to beckon me into the darkness of the unknown.

Some of my stories about death are hopeful and bright. Others are dark and border on the nihilistic. In the end, I have no idea what's going to happen to me when I die, and that makes me afraid.

Alone

Philosophers have pondered it. Theologians have pontificated about it. Scientists have been skeptical of it. Life after death. The great beyond. Sarah had been afraid of it. Then she slipped silently into it during the night.

She had no idea how she'd met death. She could only remember waking in a dark place, unable to move her limbs, because she had no limbs to move. Her nature—her mode of being—had been turned on its head in an instant. It took her ages to come to terms with the loss, to begin exploring the depths of her insubstantial self.

When at last acceptance came, she drifted through the cosmos, ready to begin whatever journey lay ahead. Moving was not so much an act of the body as it was an act of the will—a projection of thought and mind.

She called out, hoping to find others like herself, but no one answered.

Was that what death was, to be alone? The thought terrified her. If her eternal vocation was to exist in such a state, she'd rather the darkness had consumed her.

She continued to skid through the universe, crying out in increasingly panicked outbursts.

Hello? Is anyone there?

She felt her soundless voice reverberate, ripple out through space and time. But again, there was no reply. If she kept this up, she was certain she'd go mad.

Had she gone to Hell? As she streaked through a thousand worlds in silence, she pondered this terrible prospect.

Hell. Was that the reward she'd earned in life? She tried to remember, but could not. Her old life had faded until it left only the vaguest of impressions, formless shadows in the dark.

Is anyone there? Please, answer me.

She projected herself farther. Farther. Like a heat-seeking missile, she launched herself as far as she could go in search of companionship.

Sarah.

A silent whisper echoed across the void in reply. Her name. Someone had used her name. At last, an answer to her call. If she had a body, tears would have poured from her eyes.

I'm here!

Sarah, follow my voice.

And Sarah did. On and on she went, zeroing in, while every so often the voice would say something new so she could pick up its trail and continue following after it.

Sarah, over here. That's it, Sarah. You've almost made it.

There was light in the distance, not the kind she had once witnessed with her eyes but something different: a radiant, all-consuming fire that warmed her essence.

Just a little farther.

The voice was close now, still separated from her by some unfathomable chasm, but close all the same.

Suddenly, the light was a searing fire that burned just to look at it.

Sarah, you'll have to jump.

I'm scared.

But she ached to pass through it, to see what was in store for her on the other side. Most of all, she longed for communion with the voice that had reached out to her at the height of her terrible loneliness.

Just let go and jump.

Sarah felt power mounting inside her. Fear and desire warred with each other in greater and greater intensity until the fire in her own soul was a greater agony than the fire she contemplated crossing.

That's it, Sarah. Jump!

She did as the voice commanded. There was a timeless instant in which agony reached an excruciating peak, in which she could feel all the impurities of her former existence melted away. Then she was pure, pristine, and the fire could no longer harm her.

She was a part of the light now, and, inside of it, she could at last behold the one who'd spoken to her with a kind of awe she'd been incapable of in life.

Welcome home, Sarah.

Love filled her to capacity. The chasm had been bridged, and Sarah would never be alone again.

Balance

“**G**OT ANY CHANGE?”

The young couple before him averted their gazes and continued walking. Chris sighed, sat down beside his stolen shopping cart and watched traffic coast up and down Sepulveda Blvd.

He reached up to adjust the frayed, weather-worn beanie on his head, and to wipe a slimy streak of brown sweat from his forehead. The day was hot, and boy, what Chris would have done for some air conditioning.

Ah, well. He deserved this. He couldn't say why, since most of his life had been one misfortune after another, but, somewhere in the back of his mind, he believed he must have had his fair share of luck. Now, all he was doing was paying it back.

Balance. A sorrow for every joy, a broken bone for every healthy year. It was as if the universe were run by an omniscient, omnipotent accountant with a cosmic ledger to balance before the day was out.

In fact, in a previous life, Chris had found a way to cheat that ledger, to enjoy a lifetime of good fortune without any of the corresponding bad. Or so he'd thought. Turned out, the accountant had been watching the whole time, and like a dutiful IRS agent, he'd ensured Chris would pay his debt with interest.

“Hey, Mister, got any change?”

A man in a dark flannel suit stopped, turned, crinkled his nose, and said, “Get a job.” Then he moved on, leaving Chris to wallow in the heat of Los Angeles.

Oh, did he have to pay.

At the end of his original life, Chris had sat before the Great White-Robed Bureaucrat himself.

“It appears you have a negative balance,” and Chris had just sat there in the man's office, gazing outside as other souls passed through the celestial gate and into the next life.

“There's interest, of course,” the accountant continued, punching buttons on an antiquated calculator. “And penalties.” More buttons…

Chris watched a woman with gray hair pause on the threshold of two worlds, biting her lip. An angel stepped up beside her, nodded, and, a moment later, the woman turned and went through.

“That amounts to two and a half lives,” said the accountant behind his desk, double-checking his work. “Of course,” he mused, “You really can't have *half a life*, can you? We'll just round that up to three and refund the difference when you reach the other side." And then he nodded, satisfied. "Sign here."

Chris signed and waited to be born again.

In his first makeup life, he was the child of an addict, who grew up in a crack house, became an addict himself, and spent the rest of his life rotting in prison. In his second, he was a refugee from the Middle East, denied a visa by every country that interviewed him. He died of malnutrition at age forty-five.

Absent the occasional dream or moment of déjà vu, he was never aware of his past lives. But every time he died, after his life had flashed before his eyes like an old-fashioned movie reel, there was that damned bureaucrat to remind him how much time he had left.

Now Chris was on his third life, and, unbeknownst to him, he would spend the rest of it believing his fortune was just on the other side of the horizon.

"Got any change?"

A woman looked down at him in her suit and tie, had pity, and threw sixty-seven cents into the coffee tin beside him.

"God bless you, ma'am." And he meant it.

He stared down at his day's earnings, a total of $3.27, and allowed himself to smile. Soon enough, he thought, his luck would change.

Dying Breath

"TIME TO SLEEP, LITTLE ONE." Jerome's eyes began to droop.

"Mommy loves you very much." She bent down to kiss his forehead. Then she walked back to the doorway, and paused for a moment before turning off the light and closing the door.

Jerome stared up at the ceiling, watching the shadows change shape. Too young to form cohesive thoughts, all he could do was feel the lingering love of Mommy, like a warm blanket, as he drifted to sleep.

For a moment, he teetered on the edge of the waking world. Then he plummeted and all was dark.

JEROME WOKE on a bed of straw. He was not an infant but a man, elderly and gray, with an off-white beard that stuck out of his face like a clump of weeds. It was here, in the space between time, that he could remember once again who he was.

In a far-off realm, in his true body, he lay dying in a hospital bed. But a woman—a young doctor he'd been sure he knew from somewhere, but whose face he couldn't place—had given him a special gift.

"A life for every dream," she whispered so only he could hear.

He asked her what she meant, but she only shushed him and told him to go back to sleep.

She whispered something else, a baritone rumble that swallowed the world in a primordial language that he felt more than understood. He closed his eyes. When he awoke, he found himself here, on this very same bed of straw.

Now every time he closed his eyes, he woke someplace new. He would be a different age, exist in a different year. Each step on his journey through the cosmos was a flicker, a snapshot in time. Yet a billion snapshots later, he was still drifting, with only these brief interludes in his bed of hay to remember who he was.

Someday it would all come to an end, for a dying breath could only be stretched so far and so thin. But for now, he would linger, unsure if what he'd been given was a gift or a curse.

Who would he be the next time? Jerome lay down and closed his eyes.

This piece inspired a longer short story with the same title.

From Life to Death

*C*RACK.

Thunder crashed, tearing the sky asunder. A storm of apocalyptic proportions. But Martha didn't jump as so many of her neighbors did. She'd been expecting it since she was five.

The year she died.

She set her things aside and walked out into the pouring rain. The street was nearly empty; most had gone inside when the rain started. There were only a couple folks standing in their front yards, staring up at the sky as if Hell had descended from the clouds, and Martha guessed she could understand. That last peal of thunder had packed quite a wallop.

The sky was a writhing mass of charcoal clouds, pluming like broad stone columns, blotting out the sun. Martha gazed up and tried to spot the form hidden within.

"Come out where I can see you!" she shouted. "Let me look at you!"

She glanced across the street, self-conscious in the wake of her outburst. Of course, there was Harold Vernor staring back at her. Well, let him think her a senile fool. She had other things to worry about.

A second peal of thunder, like a mortar bursting in the sky, followed by a bright, strobe-like flash. The sound set off at least a dozen car alarms.

Martha stood there waiting.

MARTHA.

"I was wondering when you'd show yourself."

Martha had been five the year she contracted pneumonia. Everybody expected her to get better, even her doctor, so it came as quite a shock when she took a turn for the worse and teetered on the precipice of death. The storm had come then, just as it came now, frightening people with its great pounding cries like artillery fire.

It had approached her on the doorway of death, and in a voice only she could hear, it offered to restore her life. In return, she would let it take her again at a future time of its choosing. The idea terrified her, but if she turned down its offer, she was sure to die. So she agreed, and she woke the following morning as if she'd never been sick.

Now, just as before, rain pelted the street in a series of rapid-fire plinks. Martha was soaked to the skin.

IT'S TIME.

"I figured as much. Can't say I've had a bad life. Had my fair share of scrapes and bruises, but I guess I came out okay in the end."

Two more explosions. Light electrified the sky.

"Anyway," she continued, "I'm ready now."

YOU ARE BRAVE.

"Not brave, just old enough to know I've had enough."

THEN COME, AND LET ME TAKE YOU HOME.

A column of light like liquid fire bolted from the sky. It struck her in the head. Martha rode that wild surge into the arms of her savior and destroyer, leaving her smoldering body behind.

His Domain

A GUST OF FRIGID night air blew past James as he wound through the park, making him shiver. Like a dream, only he knew he wasn't asleep. The world was unnaturally quiet and still. There was only the wind, sighing like a mournful spirit.

Orange lamps lit the edges of an asphalt path, but the dim illumination only seemed to hint at all the things it refused to reveal. So many dark corners and hidden shadows. Anything could be out there, watching, waiting.

The most distressing thing was that he couldn't remember why he was there. Memory was a vague thing, a thin mist that parted and evaporated whenever he reached for it.

James's eyes flitted from one shadow to the next. He licked his lips. They felt cold and dry. The wind was blowing harder now; trees swayed back and forth in a harsh rhythm. Leaves and branches played a haunting tune, a dry rasping sound.

James sensed movement on his right. He whirled, strained to hear. But there was nothing. More movement to his left, the slightest flicker at the edge of his vision. Again he whirled, and again there was nothing.

James ran. Lamps and trees streaked by in a blur until his side ached and his breath started to come in ragged puffs. He had no idea where he was going—no idea what he was running from. He only knew that he couldn't stop, that stopping meant dying.

It seemed the trees and asphalt went on forever. He could make out buildings on the horizon—a smattering of yellow-orange windows like distant stars—but running never seemed to bring him any closer.

James's heart pounded until it had become a high-frequency beat that made him feel lightheaded. Eventually he stopped, and when he couldn't catch his breath, he fell to his knees, gulping for air. He wanted to keep running, but when he tried to scramble to his feet, he only succeeded in falling to his hands and knees once again.

"Why do you run from me?"

James froze. He tried to discern the source of the voice, but it moaned and whistled with the wind so that it seemed to come from everywhere at once.

"They all do, you know. They all believe they can escape. They think that if they run fast enough, that if they run long enough, they can get away, that they can cheat me out of what's always been mine."

The wind was now whipping at James's hair and clothes in a violent gale.

A figure emerged from the shadows: not from a place of hiding, but from the shadows themselves. It loomed over him, wearing the blackness like a cloak.

James wanted to scream, to summon anyone who might be close enough to help. But whatever sound he'd wanted to make had gotten caught in his throat. Finally, in a hoarse whisper, he said, "Who are you?"

"Yes," the figure mused in that same elemental voice, "and they always ask me the same thing. Who am I? Why have I come? And you know, they all know the answer before they even ask. Deep down, they've always known the answer."

The figure knelt before him, and as he leaned in with a face that was shrouded in darkness, the air grew colder. "Have you figured out who I am yet?"

James had lost most of his body's warmth. He shuddered, hugged himself with shaking arms. "Death."

"Yes."

James's vision blurred around the edges.

"You've come to take me," said James. "Because I'm yours."

"Yes, you are."

The blackness enfolded him, blinded him.

A breeze grazed the surface of his left ear like a kiss. "Death is my domain."

A flicker of consciousness, like a sputtering flame, and then James went to join Death in the dark.

Redemption

Part 1.

*F*ALLING. *TUMBLING. FIRE. Burning. Screaming.*
The man woke with a start. There was still a residue of anxiety, the vague feeling that he was being pursued, but it was already slipping from his mind, and by the time he rolled over onto his side, it had left him completely.

When he opened his eyes, blackness rushed to fill the vacuum. He panicked. Had he gone blind? He groped for the edges of his mattress and instead made contact with some other smooth surface, soft and pliable, yet firm and unyielding. Where was he?

Memory tickled the periphery of his mind, but each time he reached for it, it would disappear like a mirage.

He scrambled to his feet and wheeled about, searching for something with which to orient himself. After a while, he spotted it: a pinprick of light that pierced the darkness like a white-hot needle. Its distance was impossible to judge.

Was it real? He was afraid that if he turned away—that if he did so much as blink—it would disappear into the ether.

But the light stubbornly tugged at his eyes and refused to let go of his gaze. He paused for a moment, unsure, then chased after it.

Ahead, the light grew larger and brighter.

Part 2.

*H*E WASN'T SURE how long he'd been running. The light seemed to be getting closer, yet still he hadn't reached it. He was moving as fast as he could. He'd been pushing himself as fast as he could go, but he wasn't tired, and he was too focused on getting there to even care if he was exhausted.

Flashes of memory strobed through his mind at irregular intervals. He saw a house. A flowerbed. A mailbox. He would poke at each recollection, only to discover each time that it was a dead end.

When the light finally took form, he stopped. Suspended in the darkness was a simple wooden door, slightly ajar. Bright white light spilled out from around it and was swallowed by the blackness beyond.

He approached the door slowly. He reached out to examine it, and when he caught sight of his arm in the light, he was struck with wonder. It was the first time he'd seen himself since he'd woken.

His arm was dotted with tiny red welts that ran along the length of his veins. When he touched one, he found that it was tender.

After a failed moment searching for a corresponding memory, he glanced back up at the door. He placed his hand beneath it and verified that there was nothing to hold it up. Then he tested the sides a few inches beyond the frame and found that they, too, were empty. He walked around, and when he came to the other side, he discovered that the door was gone. He panicked, came back around, and was relieved to see that it had reappeared.

Madness.

Where did the door lead? He wasn't sure what would happen if he entered, but there was nothing for him here, only emptiness for as far as the eye could see, as if the world beyond the door had never been defined.

He gazed at the opening, hypnotized by the light. He had no choice. For better or for worse, it was clear that he was supposed to enter. He took hold of the knob, a ball of cool brass that sent a chill down his spine, and he pushed the door the rest of the way open.

The man walked forward and was consumed by the light.

Part 3.

THE MAN STOOD in the middle of a spacious living room, and he wasn't entirely sure how he'd gotten there. He knew only that he'd entered through the front door. A tiny worm of recollection niggled at his brain, but all he could dredge up was a black void where memory should have been.

Light streamed through the windows, framed by white semi-transparent curtains. Ahead, picture frames hung on a wall above a brown leather couch. Had he been here before?

He glanced down at himself. Clutched in his right hand was a worn stuffed bear with one of its eyes coming out of the socket. Where had that come from?

He ambled toward the couch, glanced up at the rows of photographs. Each one portrayed a little girl at a different stage of development. In one, she was being pushed by an older man in a car-shaped stroller. In another, she beamed up at the camera from a teal beach blanket. In each frame, she wore the same enthusiastic smile, an involuntary gesture that communicated contentment and a general love of life.

A scream.

He jumped, turned toward the stairs where the sound had come from. A dark foreboding seized him, as if a part of him already knew what he would find if he followed after it. He didn't want to pursue it.

Another scream, weaker. Then a strangled, muffled cry. Then silence.

He wanted to run—to bolt back through the front door and never return. But instead, he walked to the stairs, pulled forward as if by an invisible line.

He took the steps one at a time. Each footfall triggered a flash of memory. He was a father reading a magazine on the couch. He was a mother brushing her hair in the upstairs bathroom. He was the same father rushing up the stairs two at a time after hearing his daughter scream. He was the same mother dropping the hairbrush on the floor and running toward her daughter's bedroom after hearing the same scream.

The bursts of memory became longer, more frequent, and more coherent as he neared the top of the stairs. Like a quilt, the man had become a patchwork of other lives, all converging on a tragic event that had taken place in one of the upstairs bedrooms.

He reached the top step and squeezed the stuffed bear against his chest.

He honed in on one of the doors in the upstairs hallway, and, as soon as he spotted it, he knew that that was where he needed to go. He took hold of the knob. Twisted and pulled. Walked forward.

Once again, he was consumed by light.

Part 4.

THE MAN STOOD in a girl's room, surrounded by police. They'd cordoned off a section of space near the bed. Sitting with their backs against the wall were a man and a woman. The woman was crying into the man's shoulder. The man, also crying, held her in the crook of his arm.

On the floor by the bed was a chalk outline. Only, when he turned away and looked back again, it had been replaced by a body: the body of the young girl he'd seen in the photos. He wanted to look away, but his eyes had affixed themselves to hers.

The girl looked like she was asleep, except her head was tilted at an unnatural angle and her eyes were open, glazed, and unfocused.

He squeezed the bear against his chest.

He felt so much, a dimension that could not be perceived through the eyes but only through the heart. The room was pregnant with terror and loss, hatred and despair. The emotions writhed as if they were alive. They beat like a heart. With each pulse, the man felt as if he'd been punched squarely in the chest.

Who could have done this?

He tried to speak—to grab the attention of the couple and the officers. But neither group acknowledged him. It was as if he were speaking from the other side of an unbridgeable chasm.

He bent down beside the girl and gazed into her lifeless eyes. So young. A tragedy. He wanted to join the man and woman in their mourning. He reached out, touched a strand of the girl's hair.

A bolt of something like electricity flowed into him. He twisted and convulsed.

A flash of light and he was the girl, lying in the bed. She heard a sound outside and woke with a start. She clutched her bear against her chest, prayed that whatever had caused the sound would go away. Then she heard scraping at her window. There was a shudder, a click, and the thin layer of glass that separated her from the outside world came undone.

A man dressed in dark clothing slipped through the opening. A stench filled her nostrils. She gagged and failed to suppress a cough.

The man turned toward her. When he met her eyes, his own widened. She tried to scream, but he'd already pounced, had already grabbed her throat. All the while, that horrible odor assailed her.

There was a moment of disorientation. Thought and vision split into two.

He was the girl staring up at a strange man, the life leeching out of her as she clutched feebly at her throat. He was also the man, a junkie without money, in desperate need of a high.

All the girl wanted was for her parents to rescue her, to hold her, to tell her they loved her and that everything would be okay. All the man wanted was to stop the girl from screaming, to get out of there before the cops were called and he was sent to prison.

Her world went dark. He felt her body crumple in his hands.

There was another bright flash—a solar flare of white—and once again he was just the girl. She stood above her body, looked on with confusion as her parents burst through the doorway. They found her body on the ground. Ran to her. Cried out in disbelief.

She shouted at them, tried desperately to tell them she was okay, that she loved them. But they couldn't hear her. Then a light appeared, a tunnel perpendicular to space and time, and she was drawn toward it like a moth toward a flame. She went to it, allowed it to consume her whole. It was the most natural thing in the world to do, as natural as breathing…

The electric current ceased and the man collapsed face-first onto the floor. He was himself once more.

He'd killed her. He remembered now. The red welts that ran up and down his arm, they were needle marks, and the bear was what she'd been holding when he'd snuffed the life from her. Revulsion wracked him in waves, and he curled into a ball and sobbed like a baby. How could he? What had he done? He deserved Hell. He was the apotheosis of Hell.

A voice, addressing him by name.

He sniffed, opened his tear-streaked eyes, and looked up.

Part 5.

HE DID NOT SEE the ceiling of the bedroom, but stars in a moonlit sky. He pushed himself to his knees in a dark alley. There was a stench, foul and sour. It was a smell he'd once grown accustomed to, a smell he'd almost forgotten.

Crumpled against a concrete wall to his left was the slumped figure of a man. He crawled toward it. He lifted one of the man's sleeves, examined with almost clinical detachment the needle marks on the man's arm. He searched the chest for signs of breathing and found that it was still. The man was dead.

"You died there," said a little girl's voice.

He turned.

"The same night. I watched it happen."

Yes, he could remember now. Trembling, he'd stumbled into that forgotten pocket of concrete and asphalt, feeling like shit. He'd administered an extra-potent dose of heroin. It had been his last high.

The girl, though young, shone with an ageless wisdom that he found difficult to bear. He averted his eyes.

"I'm ready," he said.

"For what?"

"For Hell. That's where you've come to take me, isn't it?"

The girl stepped forward—he watched the pink plastic edges of her shoes glisten in the moonlight—and pulled him up by the chin.

"Is that what you want?"

"It's what I deserve."

He stared into her eyes. The girl, by way of reply, knelt beside him. He closed his eyes, prepared himself for what would come. He didn't expect what happened next.

The girl pulled him into her arms and embraced him like a mother. Emotion swelled, a tsunami of sensation that nearly drowned him. He sobbed and wailed and moaned like a lost child, and the whole time the girl held him, cradling his head against her small shoulder.

When at last the storm subsided, she pulled away. He wiped his nose with the back of his hand and gazed up at her, unable to comprehend such reckless and unconditional love.

"You were desperate. You were a slave to your addiction."

"There's no excuse for what I did."

"No," the girl agreed. "There isn't. There is love in you, but it's tarnished, impure. It must be cleansed. Justice and love demand it."

"What does that mean?"

"It means you'll have to do this again."

"No," he said when he realized what she meant. "I can't."

"You have to. You must confront your evil and the pain it's caused, over and over again, until, little by little, your spirit is broken. It's your punishment and your redemption. You must be broken before you can be made into something new."

"How long?"

"As long as it takes. Some go through it only once. Some for much longer. Some never find their way through." She gave him a warm and reassuring smile. "You've been at it for a while. I think you're almost done."

He looked up, and when he did he spotted another door, just like the first, standing a few feet away from him in the alley. There was fire and pain beyond the threshold. He could feel it. It would burn him, consume him whole.

"The fire is necessary," said the girl, as if sensing his thoughts. "It burns away the impurities. Your soul will be smelted and refined until it's been reduced to love, and when that's done, you'll find rest."

He felt a different emotion then, one he'd not experienced before. Hope. It overcame him. There would be fire, and it would hurt. But then there would be healing, and he would be made whole. He would atone, and then he would find peace.

He pulled himself to his feet. Gritted his teeth. Walked forward.

"I'll be waiting for you," said the girl behind him, "to greet you as a friend on the other side."

He opened the door. Stepped through.

He was consumed by the light.

This piece was originally broken up into a five-part serial, and I've chosen to preserve the separation.

The Man with No Name

A RIBBON OF PIPE SMOKE curls into the air. Not for the first time, I think of my grandpa, who would sit at the back of a musty kitchen, puffing his pipe, pondering a world that passed him by long ago. The memory is vivid, visceral, and it almost sends me sprawling into the distant past.

The man who sits before me now, the Man with No Name, is not my grandpa. He died eleven years ago. Though the Man with No Name would have been around when my grandpa was still alive, as well as when his grandpa was still alive. He gestures to me with his pipe before returning it to his mouth.

"Sit, Michael."

I do as I'm told. I have no idea why he's summoned me. I only know I was home, heading upstairs for bed, and when I reached the top, I realized I was no longer ascending the wooden steps in my house, but the ancient wrought-iron steps that lead to his personal chambers. Yet I've learned in all our dealings not to ask questions but to listen. He always has his reasons, and my family and I have come to trust them.

The candelabra that hangs from the high, stone ceiling glows a flickering orange. It makes me feel as if I've crossed the threshold into another world. For all I know, I have.

"Michael, I'm going to get right to the point. I'm dying."

Dying. It took a moment for the meaning of the word to resolve.

"But how?" I can't believe what I've just heard.

"My kind live long by your standards, but contrary to what you and your family believe, I am not immortal."

I feel as if everything I've been taught has been a lie. All of Grandpa's stories about the Man with No Name, about how he helped the family, once poor, to prosper and succeed. He was not just a saint to us, he was a god. Now I'm learning that even a god can die.

"Don't look at me like that."

I must have been staring. I gaze down at my feet, crestfallen. The world falls apart around me. I feel like throwing up.

"I served your family long before it had a name, but now my life draws to a close and I'd like to put things in order before I go."

"But, what will we do without you? We've relied on you for so long. I don't know how we'll survive."

The Man with No Name leans back. A grimace sours his features like rancid milk.

"I spoiled you. I should have been more discerning in my aid. Ah, well, that's love. Michael, there comes a time in every person's life when they have to leave the protection of their parents and strike out on their own. This is true of children, and it is also true of families. I've been with your kin for more than a thousand years, teaching and guiding. Now it's time to take what you've learned and make something of yourselves."

"You can't leave us."

"I have no choice. My time in this world is finished. I'm ready to flee the shackles of my body and discover what lies beyond."

Shock begins to thaw. Despair takes its place.

"Make me proud, Michael. You and your family are capable of great things. You no longer need my help, and you haven't for a while."

"But I don't want you to go." My voice cracks.

"I know."

The Man with No Name opens his arms, and I find myself running into his embrace. I cry. The arms close around me.

"Goodbye, Michael."

When I pull back, I'm standing once more at the top of my own stairs. For the first time in my life, and in all the centuries of my family's life, I know what it truly means to be alone.

The Apocalypse

Introduction

The Apocalypse. Literally the revelation of hidden knowledge, the word has become synonymous with the end of the world. It's an idea that holds a great deal of power over us. We explore it endlessly in novels, movies, and documentaries. The end of the world is something that both fascinates and frightens us, in part, I believe, because the end of the world is intimately related to our own personal deaths. The world, like our lives, is bound by the constraints of time, and, therefore, had a beginning, and will, at a time hitherto unknown, come to an end.

Some ascribe a religious significance to it. Others accept it as a theoretical inevitability. Wherever you are on that spectrum, I'll bet you've imagined the scenario at least once. Perhaps you've found yourself lying in bed in the middle of the night, asking, "Will the world end? How? When?"

We can hope and pray it won't occur during our lifetime (though with nuclear and biological weapons in the hands of our world leaders, who can say?), but then we still have to contend with the fact that someday, we're going to die; someday, each of us is going to have our own personal apocalypse.

That's a frightening realization.

End of Days

I TRIED TO STOP THEM.
I failed.

An entire world reduced to ash. The memory haunts me still. I would pray for death, but I'm immortal and cannot die.

I saw them coming when the universe was only a baby wrapped in swaddling cloth. Once they'd been my companions. But when I tired of death, I turned my back on them. I was troubled that they'd followed me, and knew someday I'd have to stop them. But they were still far, and as the cosmos matured, I was caught up in caring for it, in helping it to thrive.

I was most fond of Earth. The humans, though quick to anger and capable of great evil, were nevertheless a noble race. Quirky and extravagant, yet I fell for them just the same. If I could have, I would have forfeited eternal life in exchange for theirs.

Again, I saw them coming, those demons of ice and fire, the Old Gods I thought I'd shaken so long ago, and again I did nothing. They were still a long ways off, and there was still so much left for me to do here. Humanity was evolving, and I had to help them grow; I had to steer them clear of the path that would otherwise lead to self-destruction.

Millennia passed. The universe ripened. Humanity reached its apex. I couldn't have been more proud. Then I heard their raging shouts echo across space and time—the war cries of the Old Gods—and I knew I would have to stand up to them at last.

They came in armor. They brandished weapons. The lust for death and chaos burned in their eyes. I stepped between them and the universe and said, "You will not pass."

They looked first to me, then from one to the other, sneering as if enjoying a private joke at my expense.

"What are you doing?" their leader asked. His voice rolled across the stars like distant thunder. "You were once one of us. Why would you stop us now?"

"I've cared for this world since it was an infant. Please, leave us in peace."

Centuries passed as we gazed into each other's eyes. Then their leader threw back his head and laughed.

"You are a coward," he said. "It is well that you left us."

They advanced.

"Stop!" I shouted. "I won't let you pass!"

Teeth bared, I flung myself at them. But they were too strong and numerous, and I was easily overpowered. They tossed me aside like a piece of flotsam, and that was when I heard their leader shout, "Burn it all!"

Men, women, and children wailed as the End of Days arrived, as Earth was transformed into a celestial funeral pyre. And my former companions didn't stop there. They marched through the universe, tearing everything down. I shouted after them, begged them to spare what little was left. But by the time they'd gone, nothing remained, only a barren wasteland and I, its single surviving inhabitant.

I hung my head and wept. They'd salted everything, so that nothing like humanity would spring up again.

My children. My purpose.

Gone.

Mischief Maker

NOT LONG NOW, he thinks, before the world unravels again. His mouth blossoms in a jack-o-lantern grin.

It was just by chance that he happened upon the Earth. Wandering the cosmos in search of mischief, he'd stumbled on it by accident, and he was already moving on when he caught sight of a curious thing.

They called themselves Man. They gazed up from their tiny little rock at the dawn of their existence like ants upon a mound of sand. They beheld the depth and breadth of the mysteries beyond, and, in their arrogance, proclaimed themselves to be the center of the universe.

He's dwelled among them since. He works in the shadows, just beyond the range of human perception. A master puppeteer, he tugs on their emotional strings, takes advantage of their ape-like brains, rouses them toward anger, hatred, and war.

He waits until they've nearly destroyed themselves, then watches as they rebuild, as new civilizations rise from the ashes of the old. Then, just before they've tasted true and lasting peace, he lays his fetid hands upon the Earth and gets them to burn everything to the ground again.

Each time, he allows them to carry something into the next age; some knowledge that enables them to build bigger and better weapons. Now they have nuclear and biological armaments. He grins like a spoiled child with candy, and he watches, wondering if this time they'll break the world for good.

The Dokash

I AM NOT A MADMAN.

The doctors all say the same thing, those small-minded men and women in their white lab coats and sterile, condescending smiles. They assert that I'm delusional—that I'm a danger to myself and others. Do not believe them. I've come not to do violence, but to warn of the violence yet to come.

I am their emissary. I herald their arrival, the rightful heirs of your world, the Great Masters who were here long before you were even a dollop of goo in the primordial soup. To you, I issue fair warning. Turn from me all you like. Your refusal to listen will not save you when they come.

You, who mill about in your suits and ties like cockroaches in the dirt; you, who believe yourselves the sole sovereign masters of nature; you, who gaze up at the vastness of the universe and conclude that all of it was made for you; prepare yourselves.

They're coming. From beyond the cosmos, from beyond space and time, they're coming. They'll remake the Earth in their image. Oceans will boil. Fields will blaze. Heaven and Hell will pass away. Skin will burn. Flesh will melt. And your souls, stripped of their mortal coils, will serve the Dokash.

Mind your place, pay them homage, and you will be rewarded. But do not obey, do not pay tribute and you'll be punished, made to crawl on all fours like dogs, tongues lolling, while the Dokash regard you as children who delight in pouring salt on worms and snails, until you come to prefer the kind of death in which there is nothing at all.

Hear my words and prepare yourselves. The life you know is coming to an end.

What Was Once Mine

I SEE YOU, though you do not see me. I hide in plain sight, move around and have my being before your eyes for all that they fail to discern me. I stroll along your sidewalks, drive along your roads. I watch, I wait, I endure my punishment because I must. As I sit beside you just outside your field of vision, I muse to myself in bitter mirth. If you knew that I was there—if you knew the least of what I was—you would howl in fear, foam at the mouth like a rabid dog until the madness allowed you to forget. Thinking of this, I smile, rise from my place of rest, and continue with my wanderings.

Once, I was the most powerful man in the world. More than a man. Once, when the world was new, when men hunted in packs with sticks and stones, when men ran alongside the wolves that would one day become dogs, when men fought and killed over food like wolves themselves, I ruled them all. You would not understand the things I did, the blood I spilled, the men I worse than killed. You could not understand. The horrors wrought by my wicked hands far surpass the comprehension of mortals.

I was condemned to wander the Earth until the end of time—unseen, ignored, powerless, and alone. I was to witness those I had oppressed evolve, grow in wisdom and strength, multiply, organize, conquer the world that had been mine so long ago. "A fate worse than death," they had said. They had been fools.

Patiently I wait, biding my time, watching for the day when I can seize power once again. For all their supposed intelligence, men are weak and vulnerable. Their emotions betray them, rouse them to suspicion, to hate, to war. Whatever stability they've enjoyed until now cannot last.

Lo, my hour comes with the dawn. The very knowledge that men have used for millennia to bend the world to their will shall be their undoing. With nuclear and biological weapons in the hands of over-evolved primates, the world is a tinderbox, waiting only for that single spark to burst in flames. And when they break the world beyond fixing, I'll be there to pick up the pieces. I'll be there to remake the Earth in my own dark image.

My captors should have killed me. If they had, perhaps mankind could truly be free. Instead, the only beings capable of tearing me down lie in dusty forgotten coffins deep below the surface of the Earth, no longer capable of pulling me down when my opportunity comes again.

Enjoy your freedom, Man. Your tens of thousands of years are but a grain of sand in a swirling storm before the history of the world. All that you see before you was once mine and will soon be mine again. Enjoy your freedom, Man. It will not last.

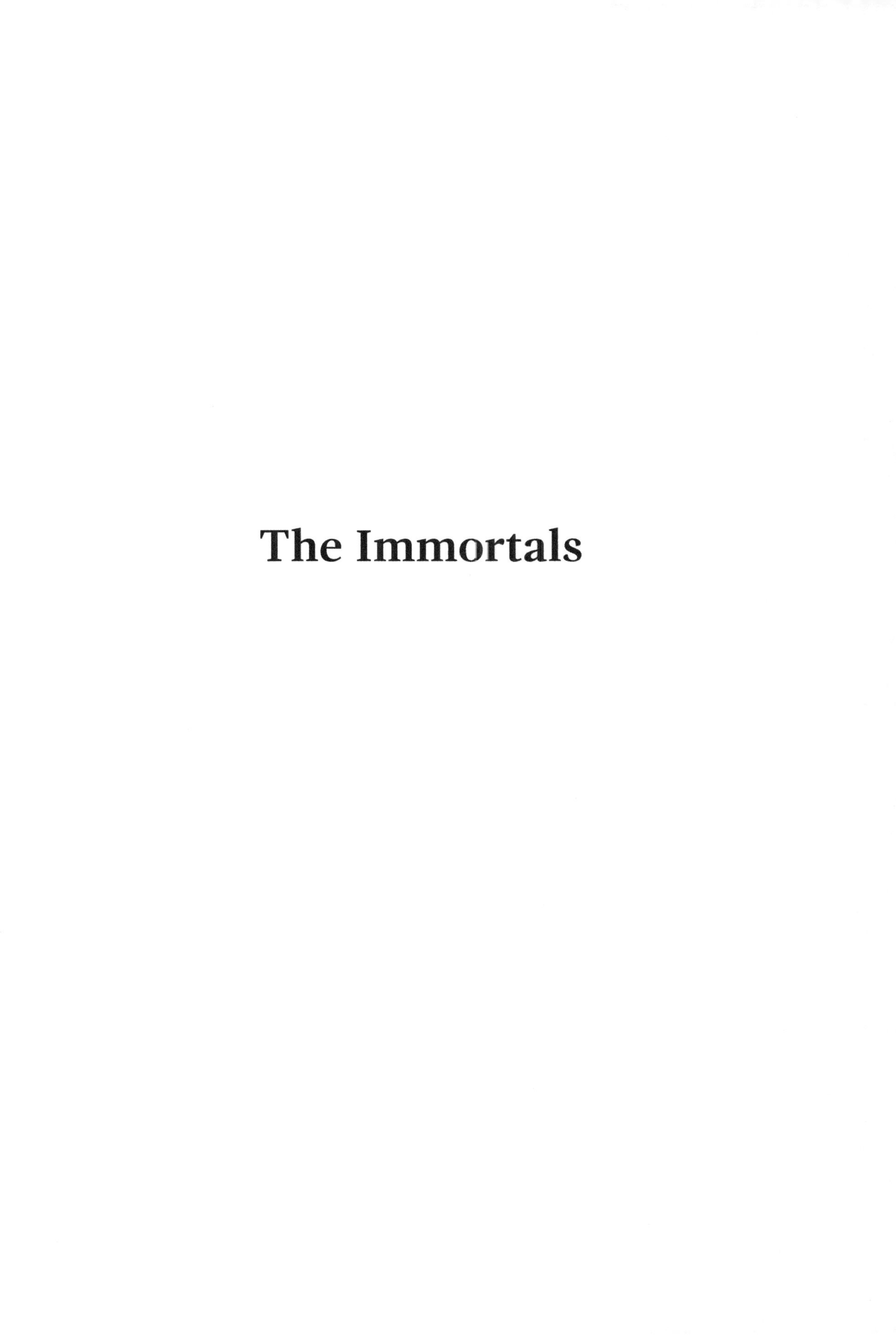

The Immortals

Introduction

The three stories in this category take place in the same universe and revolve in some way around a race of beings called the Immortals. The Immortals are guardians of the cosmos tasked with protecting space and time from a destructive horde known as the Blight (introduced in "The Tunnel.") Most of the creatures that constitute the Blight were locked away long ago where they couldn't hurt anyone, but that prison has since started to weaken.

A few members of the Blight managed to escape the Immortals when they were first locked away. They hid on various worlds, assuming physical bodies to avoid detection. In response, some among the Immortals chose to also bind themselves to bodies in order to roam those worlds and pursue the creatures where they fled. Those Immortals who also live human lives on Earth refer to themselves as Earthbound (introduced in "A Web of Ink and Paper" and later expounded on in a novella not found in this collection called *Inkbound*.) They spend their lives binding whichever creatures of the Blight they can find, and when they die, they return to their immortal incorporeal lives.

In "An Immortal in Exile," an Immortal is introduced who committed some serious crime, as of yet unknown even to himself, and who was consequently sentenced to perpetual life on Earth as punishment. His existence is similar to that of the Earthbound, with the exception that when he dies, he is reincarnated and forced to live as a human once more. It is understood by the end of this piece that his exile is redemptive in purpose, and that once he's satisfied whatever penance is required of him, he'll be welcomed home to his brethren in the stars.

I've completed two books that relate in some way to the stories found here; one is a novel called *The Stronger Half*; the other is the above mentioned novella, *Inkbound*. I'm also planning a series of novels centered around the conflict introduced in "The Tunnel." By the end of that series, the central story should be more or less complete (with the possibility of extra supplemental stories in the future).

An Immortal in Exile

I WALK ACROSS THE BEACH, following the ever-shifting outline of the water. The sun has begun to set; the sky is blossoming with fire. I watch the surf churn and froth as it rolls in and out. I find the waves contemplative. They comfort me; draw me in to myself as the water is always, inevitably, drawn back into the sea. I step into the tide on a whim, and cool briny water surrounds my legs, sometimes splashing as high as my knees.

I stub my toe on a rock and a sharp staccato curse escapes my lips. It tears me away from my center, and, for a moment, I wonder at the fragile nature of my body. I look down, spot a chunk of granite half-buried in the sand, and pick it up. I hold it toward the light, examine the structure closely. I was there, I think, when it was formed; when the Earth itself was just a rock hurtling through the cosmos. I toss it back into the ocean and watch it land with a plop.

I try to remember the distant past, and sometimes I can almost glimpse the life beyond. But so much of who and what I am is inaccessible to me. I am an ocean, of which my humanity is only a remnant small enough to be caught in a glass jar. Like Jesus in the New Testament, I have a dual nature. I am both human and divine.

I have assumed many forms, have lived many lives spanning the gamut of time and space. Like light through a prism, I have been split apart, reduced to a broken spectrum of partial selves. I have inhabited countless worlds, existed as many species, loved and lost a thousand times for every star that's ever burned in the sky.

I drift from one life to the next, a cosmic vagrant, the fullness of my being always just out of reach. I only know what I need to fulfill my current life's purpose. I must regard everything else as a mystery.

I am an Immortal, but, before the gas clouds of this universe had even condensed into stars, I was exiled. The scope and nature of my crimes are lost to me, incomprehensible to my present form. I only know that I must atone. I strive in each life to make my brethren proud, because I know they're watching and await my return. I know that someday I will redeem myself, that there will come a time when I will finally die my last death.

A wave rolls in, this one particularly strong, and I panic as I picture the sea preparing to swallow me whole.

I often imagine ways that I could die. It amazes me that after so many lives on so many different worlds, I could still fear something so banal. But my frail human psyche has bound me hand and foot to the dictatorship of instinct, and I must endure the biological imperative to survive like everyone else.

During the night, I write. It's the only way I can confront the shadows that haunt me in the small hours—the only way for me to give them form and expression. It's my way of capturing remnants of who I was. Yet words are imprecise, and there are so many thoughts that are inexpressible, transcendent, atoms of being that predate my humanity.

I gaze up. The sun is gone now, the sky transparent to the cosmos. I drink it in, eternal mysteries that are no longer mine to understand. I utter a silent prayer, a plea for mercy that I hope my kind will hear, and I accept by faith that they do.

A Web of Ink and Paper

GILES SITS IN A CORNER near the back, wearing a dark fedora. He watches as a man enters the coffee shop and places an order for a grande Americano. He waits for the man to hand over his money and receive his change. He follows the man with his eyes as he makes his way to a seat near a distant window.

The man is not actually a man at all, but something else. Something dangerous.

Giles reaches into his pocket, produces a faded leather notebook and silver fountain pen, and begins to write. He works carefully, starting with the coarser, superficial details, and slowly works his way to the more refined. They are special words. Words of power.

Giles does his best to capture the essence of the man, though even words such as these are only crude approximations. They reach inside and bind him; they pair with flesh and bone and spirit, tearing him out of space and time like a coupon from the local newspaper.

It isn't until he's nearly finished that the man by the window notices, and by then he's already fading like an overexposed negative. He bolts from his seat and stumbles backward, opens his mouth in shock, ambles toward Giles like a wounded soldier.

The patrons of the coffee shop have taken notice. Some scream. Others run. More than a few gawk stupidly, cell phones in their hands. God, thinks Giles, these are the creatures he's sworn to protect?

Before the man can take ten steps, he's already disappeared, torn from the fabric of reality and bound forever in a web of ink and paper.

Giles caps his pen, closes the leather notebook, and strolls to the door, ready to tackle his next assignment.

I explore more of Giles's origins and first experiences in the novella Inkbound.

The Tunnel

THERE IS A TUNNEL buried beneath the layers of the world, outside time, outside creation. It is dank and musty, pregnant with rot and decay. The walls are smeared with the stale blood of creatures extinct billions of years before the Big Bang.

It is a prison, erected to contain a race of pestilence and destruction that had once spanned the breadth of creation. They spread like cancer, defiling everything in their path with a cosmological blight that nearly brought all of reality to its knees. Entire universes fell in the attempt to take them down, and only when the Immortals came were they finally forced to yield.

If death could have stopped them, the Immortals never would have built it. But they would only have assumed another form, and their evil would have continued to dominate. The only way to protect the cosmos was to quarantine them: to lock them away forever in a tomb of stone, fortified with wards and seals to prevent their escape. The Immortals gave their very life essence to strengthen and uphold it, to keep the walls solid and substantial against their feral outraged cries.

But now the place lies in ruins, corrupted and forgotten—those who built it having moved on. When the prisoners were abandoned, they wondered if their captors even remembered they were there.

The seals weaken with the passing of the ages. In some places, they are stretched so thin that the prisoners can once more sense the outside. They scratch at the walls with insubstantial claws, and the structure gives, ever so slightly, in tiny, imperceptible increments.

Time has made them hungry. The Immortals thought starvation would break them, make them weak and vulnerable. But it only strengthened their resolve to ravage the cosmos once more.

Now they sense a breach, a rip in the fabric of their prison, and they rush at it with teeth bared, picking and tearing, prying and pulling. They work with grim anticipation.

They know the walls are about to come down.

Horror

Introduction

Nothing beats a classic horror story. I first discovered Stephen King in high school and instantly fell in love. I lost interest for a while (around the time my fling with high fantasy began), but after I had a few years of college under my belt, he was one of my very favorites once more.

I think one of the things I love so much about horror is that it allows you to explore who people are when they're pushed to the edge. Anyone can be a stand-up citizen when the world is stable and calm. It's a different story when things are falling apart. Will you be a hero and save your family when your house is invaded by flesh-eating zombies, or will you be a coward and run?

If I'm being completely honest, horror also speaks to a darker part of myself. In addition to problems with depression, I was bullied through my entire elementary school and high school life. Over time, I developed a serious case of social anxiety that, though currently scabbed over, will never completely heal. All those dark experiences led me to a place where I could identify with the horrific on a visceral level. That's not to say I would dare equate myself with people who have been through true horrors, like assault or addiction or abuse, only that in some small way, when I read about other people's struggles, I find myself reflecting on my own.

And perhaps that's why so many of us enjoy horror, because we all have struggles, because we all have demons to fight, however big or small they may be.

Afraid of the Dark

MOM TELLS ME not to be afraid of the dark. But I know better.

"There's nothing that can hurt you," she says with a smile before kissing me on the forehead and closing the door behind her. That's when I pull the covers over my head like a burial cloth and lie awake with my eyes open until I see the light again.

Once, I took her at her word and slept with the covers off. I trusted her then. I was sure that if she said something, it must be true. I'd begun to drift, to straddle the world of dreams in freedom and peace.

That was when I heard a voice.

"Christian," it said, sounding like the rustling of dry leaves.

My eyes popped open.

"Christian, come to me. We'll have fun together, you and I."

I threw the blanket over myself like a ward, praying it would be enough to protect me.

"Christian," it said again, a low susurrus whisper. "I'm here in the dark, waiting for you. Won't you come? You'll never have to sleep again. We can play, you and I. We'll have so much fun."

That was when I learned the truth, that there *are* things in the dark that can hurt you, and that mothers and fathers don't always know everything.

I didn't sleep that night, and I don't know if I'll ever sleep again.

Contagion

Dianne stood at the summit of a broad stone outcrop, jutting out at a sharp angle from the desolate land of the Mojave Desert. She drank it all in: the jagged outlines of sparsely spaced Joshua trees, the humongous brown and gray rocks, the limitless expanse of baked dirt and dried shrubs.

It was mesmerizing.

She would drive out into the desert alone as often as she could, with nothing but food, water, a sleeping bag, and a tent. She would hike during the day; during the night, she would sleep beneath the stars, trying to puzzle out the transcendental mysteries of the cosmos.

A wind gusted, sudden and fierce, sending ripples through her clothes. A cloud of dust kicked into the air, and she snapped her eyes shut a fraction too late.

"Ow…" She hissed, eyes stinging. She waited, expecting the pain to subside after a few moments. But her eyes kept tearing throughout the day.

That night, as the sun set beneath the peaks of distant mountains, her body began to ache, and by the time she lay in her sleeping bag inside the tent, she was feverish, racked by chills that nearly sent her into convulsions. She fell asleep wondering if she would wake.

She dreamed of a man, or was it a woman? Every time she caught sight of the creature, it would change. The amorphous entity seemed to manifest from the desert itself, raw, wild, and powerful.

It chased her beneath the scorching heat of the sun, until she fell to the ground on all fours and could not run any longer. Then it knelt beside her and whispered in her ear.

"Come," it said in a voice that carried across the dry convection-oven breeze. "Be one with me."

Dianne felt it brush against her lips—it's own mouth was dry, parched, and cracked like the dirt and the rocks—and then thought and sensation fused. She was no longer Dianne, nor was she this entity of the desert. She was a new creation, a synthesis of sand and flesh and blood.

The hybrid that was no longer Dianne woke the following morning, its fever broken. It rolled up its sleeping bag, packed up its tent. It got into its four-wheel drive pickup and drove back to the city, to civilization.

Humanity had spent thousands of years taming the desert, pushing it back to the peripheries of the world. Now, she would bring the desert back to them.

Dark Calling

J ACQUELINE PEERED INSIDE the smooth porcelain toilet, contemplating the depth of rusted pipes that descended far underground. What lurked in those black, hidden places? What horror existed just out of sight, waiting to take her in her sleep?

It had spoken again last night. It was the reason she left the toilet lid closed, the reason she locked her bedroom door before going to sleep. That fetid voice that sounded like the slopping of rancid meat, bubbling up from the sewers beneath what was otherwise a safe, ordinary neighborhood.

She could never remember what it said. It was like waking from a nightmare, knowing you'd been afraid, but unable to articulate why. She could only recall that rotten, murderous voice, speaking of things that made her skin break out in hives, and waking on the toilet with her pants at her ankles, staring into space, eyes vacant and dead.

Well, no more. Tonight, she would sleep on the other side of the house, as far from the bathroom as possible. She would stick a pair of earbuds in her ears and blast Metallica as loud as she could stand. It wouldn't lull her from her slumber with its dark calling this time.

That night, she lay on the couch, music blaring in the dark. The bathroom door was closed.

Freedom.

The thought was borne across the auditory hurricane of guitars and drums before descending into the bowels of an increasingly drowsy mind. Soon she was floating, melting into the void of unconsciousness, a soul without substance.

That was when she heard its voice.

Jacqueline.

That terrible sound of slapping meat.

Come to me, Jacqueline. Let me ruin you with my dark secrets.

Like a zombie, she sleepwalked through the hallway, the half-crazed voice of James Hetfield twining through her mind like a creeping vine. She stopped beside the bathroom door, dazed, hopelessly under its spell. She twisted the knob, walked inside, and was greeted by the sulfuric smell of rotten eggs.

Come closer.

It sang to her now, a jarring, unholy chorus that held her rapt, bound her to its malevolent charms.

The part of her that had worked so hard to escape its influence was now a thousand miles away. She was another Jacqueline—one who existed only at night, one who's sole purpose was to serve an ancient, forsaken master. It needed her now, and she would keep it waiting no longer.

When Jacqueline woke the next morning, she once more found herself sitting on the toilet, staring up at the tiled wall, her pants down to her ankles. The earbuds lay at her feet.

Jacqueline opened her mouth and screamed.

Death by Ice

I F JOHN DIDN'T FIND shelter soon, he would die.

It was his thirty-seventh birthday. He'd always wanted to see snow, so he and a group of friends had rented a cabin in the San Bernardino Mountains to celebrate. A huge snowstorm had swept the region the night before, leaving behind humongous drifts of crystal white.

"Let's go hiking," Alicia had said, and everyone thought it was a great idea. They donned extra layers of clothing and snow jackets, took their phones for group selfies, and resolved to be back in time for dinner. Unfortunately, John had gotten separated from the group.

"I have to go back," he'd said after only twenty minutes of walking. "I want to change into my snow boots."

"You know the way?" Alex asked.

"Of course. A quarter mile there." He pointed back behind them. If it weren't for the fact that they'd teased him for his terrible sense of direction, he would've asked for company.

Now John trudged through waist-deep snow and shivered. He'd lost the path a while ago, so that all that surrounded him were large gray rocks and towering pines. The cold had leeched through his jacket and snow pants, seeped into flesh and bone, and he could no longer feel his limbs. Was this how he would die? Would he exit this world only thirty-seven years after entering it, all because of a pair of shoes and a bruised ego?

I won't die. That's ridiculous.

He reached out to steady himself against a nearby tree and paused. How long had he been walking? Two hours? Three? He needed to rest.

No! A half mad thought bubbled out of a partially frozen mind.

Just a couple minutes. A couple minutes to rest his aching muscles, a couple minutes to calm his nerves. Then he could press on. In the back of his head, that manic voice continued screaming for him to go on. But he was no longer listening.

He dropped to his knees, rested his head against a nearby tree trunk. He reached back with numb hands to form a crude pillow, and he wondered vaguely why he couldn't feel the bark.

Just a couple minutes.

John closed his eyes.

HE WOKE TO SCRATCHING. Eyelids fluttered, and for a moment he was dazzled by the golden light that filtered between the treetops. Then he felt it again, coarse and painful. He got to his feet. His heart jumped into his throat.

John was surrounded by horned creatures twice as tall as himself, balanced on horse-like haunches and blood-soaked hooves. They reached out to him, scraping with scythe-like claws. He scrambled back. Bumped into a tree. Fell into the snow.

They closed in and began to rip skin and flesh. It was like having his heart carved out of his chest with an icicle. He cried out and coughed as his lungs hitched on the frozen air. He tried to pull away, but they'd pinned him against the tree so he couldn't move.

Each slashing claw stole more of his warmth, until his teeth chattered like machine-gun fire.

"G— g— go away," he rattled.

Slash. Cut.

He tried to fend them off with useless hands.

Slash. Cut.

Black began to creep into the corners of his vision. His arms and legs were dead, frozen weights.

Slash. Cut.

The image before his eyes constricted to a narrow white tunnel.

Slash. Cut.

Then light. Dazzling. And warmth. Suffusing. John marveled as feeling flowed back into his limbs. It was not the painful pins-and-needles sensation he'd expected, but a near instant restoration of feeling and motor control. The black that had conquered his vision dispersed. Now he could see not only the world around him but more—a whole other realm that waited just beyond the threshold of space and time. There was love, and a presence that wanted to protect him. John called out to it, and it answered.

The horned creatures shrieked, shielding their eyes against the sudden burst of light. Hooting and snorting, they staggered away.

The light coalesced, assumed form and substance. It was the most beautiful thing John had ever seen. It had come to his rescue because it loved him, and he found that he loved it in return. He was no longer afraid to die, not if the light would take him with it.

John opened himself to its embrace. He felt a tug. A pull. His body fell away, left to freeze in the snow. John gazed down with disinterest.

The light swept him up and carried him home.

Everlasting Life

DEATH HUNG ABOVE Karen's head like a dark shadow, ready to quicken, ready to smother her and snuff out her life. She remembered being put to sleep in the hospital for surgery a few weeks back. It felt like that now: no pain, only a bone-deep weariness. The sole difference was that this time, when she fell asleep, there would be no waking.

She tried to summon every scrap of her remaining strength, as if combined, these fragments might somehow compose a spark that could jump-start her failing body. But there was no fuel left for her body to burn—only the ashes of so many spent years, ready to be cast to the wind and forgotten.

Don't let me die!

The words ran over and over again through her mind, a mad litany rattled off to an unknown god.

She could no longer open her eyes, and the darkness behind them was beginning to merge with a deeper darkness, one that whispered of oblivion.

"Karen…"

Startled, she wanted to ask who'd spoken—she thought she'd been alone—but she couldn't open her mouth to speak.

"Karen…" said the voice again, cool, sterile, like windswept leaves.

Was she hallucinating? She'd read once that people on their deathbeds imagined all sorts of things, one last supernova of the senses before the brain shut down for good.

"I'm real, Karen."

Yes, she believed it, though she had no particular reason to.

"Let me help you, Karen. Let me give you back your life."

How can you do that when I'm so close to death? she wanted to ask.

"I can do all things," said the voice, as if it had read her mind. "All you have to do is ask."

A convulsive chill surged through her spine like a high-voltage current.

I want to live, she thought. *No matter the cost, I want to live. Nothing can be worse than death.*

"Granted."

Sleep, if it had weighed on her before, was now an avalanche, pelting her on the head, driving her down into endless darkness.

I imagined it after all, she thought, a mad sort of clarity coming over her at last.

If you're real, speak. Prove to me you're not a delusion.

Silence.

Speak, dammit!
Exhausted, Karen's mind collapsed into darkness.

S HE OPENED HER EYES the next morning, alert and reeling. When the doctors came in, surprised by her sudden turnaround, she asked if anyone had been with her during the night.

She'd been alone, they assured her. She must have been dreaming. They released her and sent her home.

She still had the old aches and pains, the same brittle bones that were prone to breaking if she wasn't careful how she walked, the same chronic cough. But she was grateful to be alive, to discover there were years left for her body to burn, after all.

Then, one by one, everyone she loved began to die. First, her sons and daughters, then her grandchildren, then her great grandchildren.

They looked upon her in their final days with the kind of uneasy reverence one might show to some terrible, unspeakable god. Deep down, they knew her long life wasn't natural, but, like terrified children, they were unable to articulate their fears, and instead they kept their distance from her until death had its way with them and delivered them from her sight.

She lives in a convalescent home now, far away in both place and time from where she'd once settled in another life. She sits on a rocking chair in a dark, shadowy corner, rocking, rocking, waiting for an end that will never come.

Only in that terrible half-life is she at last able to count the cost of her gift—not in fact a gift at all but a curse. Everlasting life, she thought, mad with despair.

Death would have been better.

GPS Signal Lost

"TURN LEFT ON Miraloma Avenue." It wasn't the synthesized voice of his GPS app, but that of a genuine human female.

Richard obeyed and turned left. He no longer questioned the GPS's choices.

"In one point two miles, turn right onto North Kraemer Boulevard."

According to his phone, he was only ten minutes away. Sweat popped from his forehead in tiny pearl sequins. He hoped he wouldn't be late. No, he didn't think he would be. That was the damnedest thing. He was always right on time. Right on time to prevent a fire, to stop a crime, to save a life. Richard had no idea where the benevolent voice in his GPS had come from, only that whenever it manifested with vague destinations like "Flood" or "Robbery" or "Suicide," it always pointed him to a dangerous event that was about to occur.

Once he'd determined it wasn't just a sick prank being played on him by one of his techie friends, he'd ignored it, driven in the opposite direction from wherever it was trying to lead him. But then he'd watched buildings burn to the ground and people dying on the news, and soon his conscience had gotten the better of him. Someone, somehow, had set him on a mission, and his heart wouldn't allow him to ignore it.

"Turn right."

Richard turned right. Seven minutes. He stepped on the gas.

He wasn't typically so anxious. Maybe at first, but the GPS had never steered him wrong. It always delivered him right where he needed to be at just the right time. But today was different. Today, the destination printed at the bottom of the screen said, "Wife."

What was going to happen to Katy? God, they'd only been married three years and had a baby on the way. He had to reach her.

"GPS signal lost."

What? Richard slammed on his brakes. A car behind him whaled on its horn and flashed its brights, but Richard didn't move.

"What do you mean, *GPS signal lost?*" Richard shouted. He sat and stared at the phone mounted to the dash, dumbfounded.

Silence. The phone's display now displayed a red banner with the text, "Searching..."
Nonono!

He had to get to Katy. Maybe if the area were more familiar, he might have guessed where the GPS was trying to take him. But instead, he'd been routed to a dingy, rundown quarter of Anaheim that he wasn't at all familiar with. Why was she so far from home?

"Tell me!" Richard shouted. "Tell me where to find Katy!"

As if in reply, the phone repeated its previous statement: "GPS signal lost."

The car behind him had swerved into the other lane and honked repeatedly until it was out of sight. Other cars were doing likewise, but Richard wasn't paying attention. Instead, he yelled. Bucked. Screamed. Banged the steering wheel with balled fists. Threw the phone against the door.

"GPS signal lost."

"No…" said Richard, weeping now. "No. Tell me, goddamn you!"

He drove for more than an hour, frantic. He almost hit three other cars as he cut corners at over sixty miles per hour, scouring the streets for signs of his wife.

He'd just pulled over to the side of the road, desperate and lost, when his phone rang. The sound startled him and filled him with unexpected terror. What did that mean? He reached for the device with hands that were now shaking and looked down at the display. He didn't recognize the number.

Slowly, as if dreaming, he answered the call.

"Hello?"

"Hello, this is the Anaheim Police Department. Are you related to Katy Aimes?"

A stone sank in his stomach. In a dull voice, he answered, "Yes. I'm her husband."

There was a sigh at the other end. "Mr. Aimes, I'm very sorry, but we have bad news about your wife."

Innocent Blood

The boy strolls through my alley alone, and I bare my gums behind the shadows. I was like him once. More than a thousand years ago, I would lie beneath the stars and dream of far-off places. I was a bundle of youthful optimism and endless possibilities.

That was before I changed.

I'd strayed from our clan's caravan and was playing in the woods when I stumbled on an old woman sitting atop a pile of gray stones. She was crying. I asked her what was wrong, and she answered that people were selfish, and that there was no such thing as love. In my childish idealism, I proclaimed that she was wrong. She sneered, insisted I was a foolish boy, said that I knew nothing of the world and its ways.

I stood firm in my convictions.

She asked about my family, asked if they would still love me if I were different. I nodded vigorously, echoed what I had been taught by my mother and father, that blood and clan were everything.

"All right," she said. "Let's see."

She stood, gnarled and ancient. She was hunched at the back, yet she managed to tower over me. She held out her hands, closed her eyes, and, in a language I did not know, she began to speak.

A breeze stirred, a rustling of dirt and leaves that seemed to rise up from the Earth. It cut through me, spoke to the different parts of me, and commanded them to change. Skin became fur. Teeth became fangs. I fell to all fours in disbelief.

"See if your family will take you back now," she said, and she laughed, a wild cackle that made my chest grow cold.

I loped back to my village, stumbling as I learned to control foreign limbs. I found my family's tent among the caravan and called out to them. When they came outside, I tried to tell them what had happened. But only animal sounds escaped my muzzled throat. At the sight of me, they roused the clan and fetched their weapons. I was forced to flee into the night with stones and arrows at my back.

I had lost everything: my mother and father, my brothers and sisters. I kept trying to return, but every time, they chased me away. I stalked the woods, searched for the old woman so she could change me back.

I never saw her again.

The years that followed hardened my heart. I prayed for death to take me—to put me out of my misery—but, in her cruelty, the old woman had made it so I couldn't die. Instead, I wandered the world, and all the while the world changed.

Now, I prey on innocent blood because I'm jealous of what can no longer be mine. I tear their throats out with powerful canine jaws, and I delight in their blood as it drains from their faces to spatter the ground beneath my paws.

The boy stops beside me and I grin, open my maw and prepare to pounce.

Leaves in the Wind

A DRY RUSTLE makes Nicholson turn. Leaves, caught up in a breeze, gliding lazily across the sidewalk before settling back to the ground. The muscles in his neck and shoulders tense.

Just leaves. Relax.

He turns and continues down the street.

Not a big deal, he thinks, though he's started to walk faster. It happens every October. The leaves fall, dry like shed snakeskins, and are blown about by the wind along the street.

Once more, he can hear them behind him, skidding across the concrete, a hollow rattling whisper.

Nicholson turns again. The wind is still gusting, and the leaves, suspended in the air, twirl and dance as if alive.

As if alive.

Nicholson bolts. This is silly, he thinks as he picks up speed. The spirit he encountered all those years ago is long gone, a forgotten phantom that Nicholson escaped decades past.

Only it isn't silly. He's had too much experience with his old nemesis to think it's a coincidence.

The leaves stop and he glances back. It's toying with him, playing on his fears. He slows, then stops and gasps as he catches his breath. Running, he decides, won't do him any good. His only defense all these years has been to keep a low profile, and now that defense has been shot to Hell. Nothing left to do but face it head on.

"Nicholson." The voice comes out a dry, dusty whisper. "I told you you couldn't avoid me forever."

The wind kicks up around him, forming an invisible wall, tugging at his shirt sleeves, tousling his short, sandy hair.

"How did you find me?" Nicholson asks.

Leaves dance around him with delight.

"I am the wind. I am everywhere." The breeze grows louder, stronger. "You are free because I let you go, not because you could have escaped me on your own."

"Then why did you let me go?" Nicholson tries to sound defiant, but can only manage a strangled croak.

The wind has become a tornado.

"Because I enjoyed watching you run. Because you were always looking over your shoulder, terrified of every breeze, every rustling leaf. But I'm tired now, and hungry, and in the end, even amusing prey is just prey."

Nicholson's shirt brushes against the spinning wall of air and the fabric tears, yanked away to become part of the raging tempest.

Nicholson's eyes open wide in preternatural terror.

"Goodbye, Nicholson."

The wall closes in.

Nicholson screams.

London Bridge Is Falling Down

H E BOARDED THE TRAIN from Brighton Station at two forty-five, clutching a black leather briefcase. The car was crowded, but he found a seat at the back and made his way toward it. He sat down next to an elderly woman, who glanced up and smiled. He returned the gesture and idly wondered if she would be alive tomorrow.

An artificial female voice came over the loudspeaker, notifying the passengers that they were on the Southern service to London Bridge and that their next stop would be Preston Park. It would take an hour for him to reach the last station. He settled into his seat and gazed outside as the train pulled away from the platform with a dull electric hum.

He could remember when the trains had run on steam and not electricity. They'd been much louder then, always hissing like angry spirits just before leaving the station. But that was a long time ago.

He heard the voice of a child and turned. It was a boy of six or seven, telling his mother what he'd done in school. The woman beside him smiled listlessly in most of the right places. He wondered if she would have appreciated the moment more if she knew it might be their last.

To him, humans were curious creatures. They always took what they had for granted, until it was snatched away. They were like spoiled children, capricious and short-sighted, and every so often they needed a catastrophe to wake them up and remind them of how fragile "ordinary" life truly was.

He and his companions had been working in the shadows since the Earth was a flaming ball of molten rock. Always they would wait for humanity to reach a certain level of sophistication, then tear civilization down and watch as the humans scattered like frightened ants, scrambling to rebuild.

Sometimes they directly intervened, sparking natural disasters like the one that cast Atlantis into the sea. More often, they would simply plant seeds of discord during brittle moments in history and let nature take its course. Such had been the case during the fall of Rome, the sacking of Constantinople, the Holocaust, even the rise of ISIS in the Middle East.

He glanced at the suitcase by his feet. If only the passengers in the car with him could see what it contained. The item inside would raze civilization to the ground, plunging the world into a second Dark Age.

When at last he reached the station, he caught himself humming the tune of *London Bridge Is Falling Down*. He smiled when he considered just how true that was going to be.

Merchant of Desire

HE IS CALLED the Merchant of Desire.

He operates in a dingy stucco-walled strip mall and has been in business for as long as anyone can remember. Only the foolish or the desperate seek his aid, and then only as a last resort. They're people without ambition, people who hate their jobs, their spouses, their families; people who've gone mad in the wasteland of routine.

They appear in the dusty doorway without appointments, and an electronic bell chimes when they gather the courage to enter.

They inch forward into the dark environment, anxiety knotting their stomachs as they pass through a mostly empty building that appears long abandoned.

The Merchant waits in the back. He wants the unsettling nature of the shop to work on their minds. Only the most desperate stay, and it's only the most desperate who interest him.

When enough time has passed, he steps out from behind a dark curtain and announces himself in a sudden flourish that makes his patrons jump. He apologizes, offers soothing gestures and comforting words.

He is the consummate salesman.

The anxiety doesn't escape them completely, but after a joke or two, perhaps a few words about the weather, they start to relax. They allow the Merchant to charm them with his hospitality, knowing full well he's a dangerous man who can't be trusted. He listens to all they have to say, and he regales them with tales of his own life—of his youth in rags or his youth in riches, of growing up an only child or growing up among five siblings.

As they listen, they let their guards down, so that eventually each discloses something compromising. A sibling's habit they find annoying. A regret that keeps them up at night. Unsettling dreams. Tiny cracks in the psyche reveal themselves, and the Merchant prods with great care until the window dressing that covers their naked souls has come undone without their having realized it.

They open up to him then, forgetting all about his reputation. They reveal that their lives have been affectations, pretenses of passion constructed daily to hide the apathy that's consumed their hearts, reducing them to gnarled, withered stumps. They ask how such a thing could be so—if there's something wrong with them, if something's not right in their heads.

This is the opportunity the Merchant has been waiting for.

By this time, his soon-to-be customers have made up their minds. For mere dollars, he offers them ambition, dreams, desire. He offers the opportunity to feel once more, to escape the icy prison of indifference that's tormented their malnourished souls for so many years.

They're skeptical, of course, at least on the surface. They invariably call him mad, absurd, even disingenuous. But in the most primal regions of their hearts, they know he can give them what they think they want.

He always has his way with them in the end.

He leads them to a dark, windowless room in the back. He sits them down in a corner on a small wooden chair. He tells them to close their eyes, then hovers over them unseen, where he reaches into their minds.

He navigates the labyrinthine corridors of their psyches with ease, wending his way through broken dreams and broken hearts. He knits and mends, constructs new dreams from the detritus of the old.

His customers wake refreshed and invigorated. They rediscover purpose. Each finds their mental compass has been reoriented. The Merchant bows and wishes them the best of luck.

But there's still the matter of the price.

To start, there's a modest financial exchange. This allows the Merchant to pay his rent. But his rate is low and his customers are always surprised.

There's also a hidden fee, one his patrons never see coming. It usually costs them their lives.

Most don't last for more than a few years. Their ambitions outgrow their accomplishments and they find they can never be satisfied. They don't blame the Merchant. Why would they, when the fault lies solely within themselves? They believe their goals are reasonable and they can't understand why they're unable to achieve them. If only they'd worked harder. If only they'd put in more hours. Saved more money.

They push themselves until they've depleted what little energy they have left, and the Merchant watches from a distance, feeding on their ballooning ambitions like a vampire.

Some commit suicide. Others suffer heart attacks and strokes. A few survive to old age, but only as desiccated husks, devoid of anything beyond a heartbeat and a pulse.

The Merchant always regrets their passing. If only he could feed on them forever. But there are always others to sustain him.

It's never a hard sell.

Prey

A shadow grazed the surface of the wall. Jackson whirled, momentarily dazzled by the piercing gold of nearby streetlights. Nothing. Rivers of sweat flowed down the tiny crevices of his age-worn skin, while his heart pounded out Morse code. He was prey. That knowledge propelled him into the night.

A flash of memory like a strobe. Mom and Dad, cradling him in their arms, the reflection of a past love so strong that tears began to mingle with the sweat. How he missed them. He'd been safe then. The world had been safe.

Another shadow, glimpsed from the corner of his right eye. Once more he whirled. Once more, nothing. He knew he wouldn't see it coming, that even if he'd been looking straight at it, he'd have only seen a blur of color here, a lessening of light there. The Wanderers were amorphous. That was why it was chasing him, to steal his body. They were like supernatural hermit crabs, except they didn't wait for the owner of the body to die before snatching it for themselves.

Jackson turned a corner, sprinted until he nearly slammed into a concrete wall. A dead-end alley. Fuck, he'd turned in to a dead-end alley!

Nobody knew what the Wanderers were nor why they'd come, only that one day they'd invaded en masse to blanket the world in darkness. Civilization hadn't completely unraveled, at least not yet—humanity was strong; Jackson had faith it would endure. But, like Jackson's life, it was on the brink.

He clawed at the far wall, forced himself to turn, and there, standing before him, a vision of darkness only half-glimpsed. Even in the night it was visible, an inkblot on the surface of the world that shifted before his eyes every time he tried to get a clear reading. He stumbled forward, bumped into another wall, stumbled forward again. Then he tripped over a concrete brick and went flying into the asphalt.

Pain, bright and flaring. Vertigo seized him and he felt like throwing up. It was upon him now; he could feel it. Not a physical weight, but a heavy burden nonetheless, coiled like a snake, ready to strike.

On the precipice of death, he saw who he was reflected through the viewfinder of eternity. Then it lunged and the world went dark.

Tainted Eyes

THEY SAY YOU can see it first in the eyes, a blue tint in the whites like colored contacts. A day or two later, the madness sets in. Nobody knows what it is or where it came from. If they'd had more time to study it, they might have figured it out.

Now, blue-eyed monsters roam the streets at night, breaking the world—creatures that were once our fathers and our mothers, our sons and our daughters. Though human in appearance, they're only hollow shells of their former selves, dark monuments of loss erected by an unknown disease. Not the zombies of pop culture, who prowl the remnants of a post-apocalyptic world. Something else. Something worse.

Nobody knows how it spreads, only that more of us turn each day, that any one of us could become the monster we fear. If tomorrow you wake with tainted eyes, make your peace with God and pray we put an end to you before the madness does it for us.

Taxi

S TEVE STOOD BY THE SIDE of the road, his arm extended. He was hailing a taxi. The street was filled with tricycles and jeepneys, all of them honking their horns and spurting plumes of dark gray soot into the air. He'd never seen anything like it, not until his first trip to Manila last year.

This was now his third time in the Philippines. He'd booked a condo in Quezon City for two weeks through Airbnb to see his girlfriend, a rehab doctor he'd met online. Now, he was on his way to her apartment.

Almost fifteen minutes passed beneath the sweltering tropical sun before a white MGE taxi pulled over to meet him. He opened the right rear door and addressed the driver.

"Banawe? By the Orthopedic Center."

The man nodded and Steve got in. The taxi pulled back into traffic.

Steve was still unsure of himself abroad and had a lot of anxiety navigating Manila. His girlfriend had told him horror stories about foreigners being abducted and held up in taxis, and she'd warned him to be careful. He pulled out his cell phone, which now contained a Globe prepaid SIM, texted the plate number to his girlfriend, and pulled up his GPS app to make sure he was headed in the right direction.

On his left, a cluster of street children was running around half-naked in the middle of the street. Behind them, squatter buildings jutted from the ground, jagged, haphazard constructions of the flimsiest building materials imaginable.

By the time they merged onto Quezon Avenue, traffic was moving at a snail's pace. It was so much worse than LA. He'd never imagined so many cars could be packed into the same space.

"Bad traffic," said Steve.

The driver didn't respond. Steve settled back into his seat and sighed. At least the car was air conditioned.

A tiny black fly landed on his arm, and he swatted it away. He glanced down at the map on his phone, even though he'd already done so three times and knew exactly where he was.

Another fly, this time on his shoulder. Then another on his forehead, and another on his leg.

It was when he felt them getting into his ears that he began to panic. He looked up and gasped. The air inside the cab had swollen with bugs. They were buzzing all around him, filling his nostrils, drilling into his ears, reaching into his mouth.

He had to get out of the car. He tried to open the door while they were stopped in traffic, but the handle wouldn't budge. It seemed the cab had been locked from the inside.

"Let me out!" he cried, choking on flies. The driver didn't say a word.

For one crazed moment, he was certain it was a dream, that any second he would wake up in his bed to the sound of the air conditioner whooshing in his room.

He coughed and gagged on air that was becoming increasingly dense and unbreathable. A deep resonant hum rose up from the front passenger seat, and when Steve gazed in that direction, he saw something like a bloated, deformed dragonfly, floating lazily in his direction.

He kicked and thrashed, trying once more to force the door open. At one point, he started banging on the glass, convinced that if he pounded hard enough it would break and he could escape to safety. All the while, that disfigured creature drifted toward him, humming and buzzing as if it had all the time in the world.

It landed on his shoulder and Steve batted it away. Then it landed again and Steve swatted at it once more. He tried to strike the creature in the air, but it nimbly avoided him. Finally, it landed on his ear.

Steve felt it vibrate against his skin, the buzzing becoming a deep, bass rumble. When it burrowed inside, Steve squealed like a child. Never before had he experienced such world-shattering pain. It pushed and clawed and tore its way inside. There was a deafening pop as it punctured his ear drum. Then it dug into his skull.

In a fit of madness, he considered banging his head against the door. Then the world went dark.

More digging, more tearing, and then—

Steve was assaulted by thoughts that were not his own. He could hear them all, the tens of thousands of flies in the air, the driver in the front seat, blurred and indistinct, a collective consciousness born of their intersection.

It all swirled inside of him, dissolving his mind like a corrosive acid until what remained was not Steve, but something larger. The part of himself that had been distinct, the part that had made him human, was gone. Not dead, but driven into the background and put to sleep.

When they pulled up at his girlfriend's apartment, he didn't pay. Instead, he exited the car and waved. The driver returned the gesture before merging into traffic.

Steve greeted the guard and started up the stairs. He couldn't wait to see his girlfriend.

He had something to show her.

As many of my readers know, I've been living in the Philippines with my now wife since 2015. It took me a while to absorb the culture before I felt comfortable writing about the country, and this was one of my earliest forays into a Philippine setting. The name of the street is real, as is the city I lived in and the apartment where Steve goes to meet his girlfriend. I promise, though, I'm not really part of a bug-induced collective consciousness. Honest.

The Faceless Man

He wanders the world, the Faceless Man, journeying from city to city, always in search of items to add to his collection. When you answer your door, he won't say a word; indeed he cannot, for he has no mouth with which to speak. Instead, he'll incline his head, ever so slightly, all the while clutching a black leather-bound book to his chest with reverence.

He'll open to the first page, always blank, and bid you gaze upon its fallow surface. Then dutifully, curiously, you'll look to see what all the fuss is about. Before you know what's happened, you'll have been pulled inside, transformed from a creature of flesh and blood to an indeterminate being of pen and ink.

He'll take you home and place you atop a dusty shelf. From time to time, he'll pull you back down, sit in his favorite armchair to read, and drink your loneliness, your madness, your despair, savoring them like a rare vintage.

You'll never die, but you'll spend eternity wishing that you had.

The Magician's Heir

I SIT OUTSIDE, take a bite of my club supreme on white, and gaze out over the contours of my life from the other side of time. So much has happened in the intervening years, so many terrible, unimaginable things. If I didn't know better, I'd say I was a character from a novel, the dark protagonist caught up in a strange, otherworldly fantasy.

I squint up at the sun, turn my gaze to the tops of towering downtown office buildings, and size up the world around me, no longer big enough or important enough to hold my interest. I moved on long ago, and the hollow half-life of humanity means nothing to me now.

I was thirty-three the year the magician took me. Thirty-three. The number felt old then. I could already see the threat of death looming in the distance, peering at me from the shadows when it thought my back was turned. But now, in the context of eternity, it is nothing, only a mote of dust against the backdrop of the cosmos.

"You will be my heir," the magician said. It was not a question—this, after having been the man's hostage for more than six months.

"There will come a time when you'll have no choice but to accept me," he said. "You'll see."

And with time, I did.

He changed me. Not all at once, not in a blinding flash of brilliant neon light, but incrementally, a hardening of the heart here, a withering of the soul there. I thought I could resist him, that I could resist becoming like him.

But I was wrong.

He took all that was dear to me, all that I loved and valued, all that I held close to my heart, and burned it to ash.

"Are you beginning to understand?" he asked one day as he stepped over the remains of my mother's charred and tortured body, a glowing demon haloed by fire.

By this time, there were no tears left for me to shed. I said that I did, and as the flames cooled to smoldering embers he grinned, showing all of his razor-sharp teeth.

"Then come," he said, taking my hand and leading me into the dark. "I have much to teach you."

It was in the ashes of my old life that my new life began.

The Man in the Mirror

I AM the Man in the Mirror. We meet when first you wake and again before you lay your head down to dream. I am everyone, and no one.

Summoned by your gaze, I am conjured from the depths of my ancient prison against my will, forced to take form in a parody of life, a puppet bound to you by unseen strings. You twitch your mouth in a cruel, derisive smile, and I grin back, hating you for all that you are.

Sometimes you reach out to touch the mirror, as if you sense my presence beyond the glass, and I do the same, willing the wall that holds me back to let me through, to let my hand close around your neck.

Then, you leave the room and turn out the light, and I disappear once more into the formless void. Here I brood and wait in bitter anticipation for the day of my release.

After all, no prison can hold forever.

We Are You

THE CREATURE SHRIEKED. Diane ran.

Rain fell, pattering down on the street, while above, in the clouds, thunder exploded like aboriginal drums. The rain had soaked through her clothes, and a chill was settling into her chest. But she kept running, blood pounding, side aching, because something dangerous was behind her, and if she let her guard down for even a moment, she'd be dead.

Another shriek, a war cry that drained the blood from her already pallid face.

Have to go. Have to get away.

The streets had been abandoned years ago and Diane was alone. Buildings slumped around abandoned lots, while empty cars tilted into gutters and signs hung from rusted posts like ancient monuments to forgotten gods.

No one left but Diane, which meant no one left to help.

She remembered a time before the invasion, before the world had been reduced to broken structures and shattered dreams. The image most prominent in her mind was that of her mother, cradling her in her arms when she was only three. Nobody would have believed her if she'd said she could remember such a young age, but Diane recalled every word that passed from her mother's lips as she sang Diane's favorite song, every stroke through her hair as she leaned in to whisper that she loved her, that no harm would come to her as long as she remained in her mother's arms. The potent memory of what she'd had and what she lost made her chest ache.

I miss you, Mom.

Then pain shot through Diane's leg, and the world rose to meet her, knocking the air from her lungs.

The gutter. She'd tripped over the gutter. Diane staggered to her feet, eyes wide.

"No…" she whispered. "No."

But it was too late. By the time she found her balance, she'd already seen its eyes, staring at her from across the street.

Diane's eyes.

Her dark double's thoughts immediately burst inside her mind.

We are you, now. The time for running is over.

It was the last thing Diane heard.

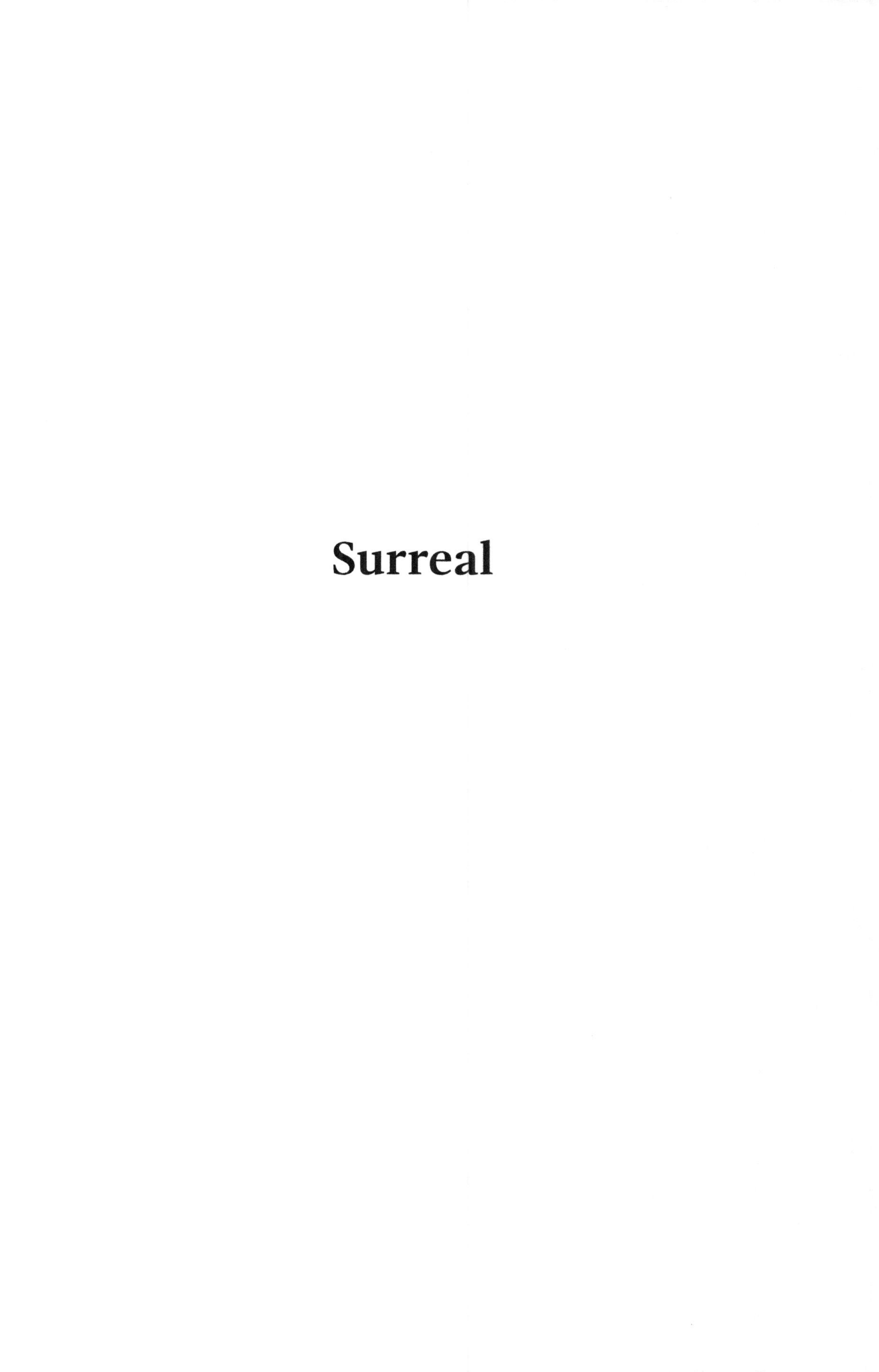

Surreal

Introduction

For the longest time, my view of the world was narrow and constricted. There were certain laws of physics that couldn't be broken, certain tenets of religion that had to be obeyed. Then I started questioning things. Suddenly, I had no idea what was true and what was not. Suddenly, the world was elastic and pliable and could accommodate almost any sort of reality at all.

That is not to say I believe that reality is subjective, or that one "truth" is just as good as any other. Truth, as far as I'm concerned, is an objective reality. But what *is* that truth? Once you ask that question, you discover almost anything is possible, that the old cliché is right: Truth really is stranger than fiction.

Now that I've been humbled and put in my place, now that I can see how small we are and how great the cosmos is by comparison, all sorts of stories become fair game, no matter how fantastical, no matter how abstract, no matter how unlike our ordinary human perceptions they may be.

Of course, all stories must in some way relate to the human experience. Otherwise, how can we understand and appreciate them? Nevertheless, I enjoy stretching that requirement to its outermost limit, because we humans are dreamers and explorers, and because if our means of traveling to the stars are still constrained, no such limitations apply to the vistas of the imagination.

Anathema

ARNOLD STOPPED TO PEER at the moon, glabrous and pale in the late night sky, then slipped through the broad cathedral doorway. The church was silent, except for the echo his shoes made when he walked across the marble floor, and he suppressed a shudder as he passed by flickering candles and confessionals that were surrounded by leering statues of the saints.

He stopped beside the front row of pews, genuflected before the blessed sacrament behind the altar, and sat. It was a ritual he'd learned in his youth. A ritual he hadn't practiced in years.

The domed ceiling rose to a spectacular height; it was covered in otherworldly frescoes depicting the cosmic struggle between God and Satan. He looked up and felt dwarfed by the vastness of eternity, a terrible awe of Heaven and Hell, and felt as if he might be crushed between the two.

Arnold took a deep breath and gazed at the altar where a large wooden crucifix loomed over the empty congregation, hidden beneath a dark shadowy veil. He imagined the figure of Christ within, his face frozen in perpetual agony.

It was Holy Week, a time of penance and reflection, and Arnold had a lot to think about.

The cathedral was a special place. Time was thin here, and if he focused hard enough, he was sure he could peer through it, into the past, where he'd spent his formative years in the Church; and into the future, where he searched for answers to questions that had almost destroyed him once and threatened to destroy him again.

What was he? He was no closer to figuring that out than he'd been fifteen years ago when his transformation began.

Life had been simple when he was a child. He'd done as his parents had told him, had believed as the priests had taught him. He'd gone to mass and confession, learned his prayers, absorbed himself fully in the truth that was presented to him.

Now, he was a stranger in his old place of worship, a stranger to his family, a stranger to himself.

He waited, as if God might glance down from Heaven and notice him at last. But there was only the quiet and the dark.

A faint buzz emanated from the stone walls, as if a tension was mounting in the cathedral's foundation. Arnold closed his eyes to pray.

"Hail Mary," he began, voice husky and dry. He stopped to clear his throat, then started again. "Hail Mary, full of grace, the Lord is with thee."

Was there a Lord? If so, how did Arnold fit into His plans? The buzz grew louder, and Arnold could feel the pew begin to vibrate beneath him.

"Blessed art thou among women, and blessed is the fruit of thy womb, Jesus."

What did it mean to be blessed? Arnold had been taught that to be saved, one must remain in a state of grace. Was Arnold in a state of grace, or was he now anathema? Did he have a place in Heaven, or a place in Hell? The buzz transfigured, became a loud shuddering rumble.

"Holy Mary, Mother of God, pray for us sinners, now and at the hour of our death. Amen."

A thunderous crack exploded like a cannon, and Arnold's eyes popped open.

The veil had torn along a jagged seam that ran down its center like a fault line in the Earth. The heavy wooden cross beneath trembled, leaned forward as if in prayer, then came crashing down, destroying the tabernacle, scattering consecrated hosts like confetti.

The Earth shook with such violence that Arnold imagined the gates of Hell were opening, ready to swallow him whole.

"Please, God, make it stop!"

Arnold rocked back and forth like a toddler, holding his hands over his ears as if the gesture could protect him.

Then—just like that—it was over. The Earth stopped moving. The cathedral fell silent once more.

Arnold's neck bulged as he beheld the desecrated altar; his veins popped to the surface of his skin like thick cords.

"What am I?" he shouted at the painting on the ceiling. "Why are you doing this to me?"

A man emerged through the open doorway behind the altar, a silhouette wreathed in moonlight. He stepped forward until the pallid illumination revealed a pair of wide, disbelieving eyes.

The parish priest.

Arnold leaped to his feet and bolted.

An Unexpected Visitor

M ARTHA GLANCED AT THE CLOCK on the wall. Eight p.m. She sighed, turned off the TV and prepared for bed.

While brushing her teeth, she gazed into the mirror, and, not for the first time, she wondered what the hell had happened. In her mind, she was still a nineteen-year-old woman, yet she now had the achy, arthritis-ridden body of seventy-five. She could feel the weight of time pressing down on her, breathing down her neck, stalking her in every unseen shadow. She never failed to be surprised by how ephemeral life seemed in these vulnerable moments, like vapor that was solid to the eye, yet evaporated to the touch.

She spat her toothpaste into the sink, rinsed out her mouth, and turned off the light.

G HOSTS OF THE PAST visited her as she tossed and turned through the night, visions of people and places that had either changed beyond recognition or were no more. The world seemed pliable in that place between dreams and the waking world, a land of impossible geometries and infinite possibilities.

It was in one of these not-quite-dreams that Martha received an unexpected visitor.

"You returned," she said when she spotted him floating by the windowsill.

"I promised, didn't I?"

"I was fifteen when I last saw you. You promised to come back, but I gave up on you by the time I was thirty-five. Why did you take so long?"

The phantom reached out with insubstantial hands. "You were young. You needed experience that only age could provide."

"Well, look at me," she said. "You got what you wanted."

"But don't you see? You are so much more lovely now."

She said nothing.

"I have something for you. Open your hands."

Martha had not seen this particular visitor in decades, yet she trusted him now and did as she was told.

"You saved us. An entire world exists today because once you loved. Now, that world belongs to you."

Martha looked down at her gift and gasped. She held the universe in the palm of her hand.

"My final gift to you," said the apparition, and then he smiled and disappeared.

156

Anya Returns

S HE STARES AT ME with eyes of purple fire, a blazing phantom in the dark. My breath catches in my throat, and when I finally speak, it comes out a hoarse whisper.

"What happened, Anya?"

The woman I had known so many years ago grins.

"My eyes were opened."

I wait for her to say more, but that's all she offers in reply.

We grew up together, Anya and I. We were best friends, inseparable from the start. Our relationship turned intimate, and, by the time we neared our college graduation, we were already contemplating marriage.

That was when she disappeared.

Now, she rolls onto her side, pressing her body against mine, and I instantly grow hard with years of pent-up longing. I have never felt an urge so strong. It overloads my synapses, drives me to the brink of madness.

This is a dream, I think. *Any minute I'll wake up.*

This close, I can see myself reflected in her spectral eyes.

Her family and I spent years looking for her. The police gave up in a matter of weeks for lack of evidence, but we kept searching, scouring her apartment for clues, interviewing her friends, calling the numbers in the phone she left beside her bed.

Now, here she is again, lying in my bed as if the intervening years were nothing.

"You loved me once," she whispers. Her breath tickles my ear. I detect the familiar smell of lavender and lilac. Her favorite scent, at odds with the feral untamed fire in her eyes.

Those flaming pupils bore into my own, extract my deepest secrets.

"I don't understand," I say, because there's nothing else to say.

"Then let me help you understand."

Her mouth opens, joins with my own. Another fire kindles, erupting to life inside my body. She leaps on top of me, hot to the touch, and I have no choice but to offer up my heart as an immolation.

"Love me now," she says, and as our bodies become one, as the embers of an old love ignite once more, I glimpse the possessing spirit within and welcome it into myself.

Embraced by the Light

"Next."

Mark's heart somersaults. He's close now, only fourth in line. Soon he'll be moving on. Every now and then, he steals nervous glances at the cavern surrounding the terminal. Inscribed on the rough stone walls are symbols whose meanings modern scholars still haven't deciphered. Above, incandescent bulbs provide a dim illumination.

There's a bright indigo burst as the portal gate slides open. He squints, watches with a sinking feeling while the person at the head of the line steps forward. For a moment, the glow intensifies. Then the gate closes and, once more, the only source of light is the bulbs overhead.

Nobody knows where the portals come from. They predate history. Perhaps they were built by a race more powerful than their own. Perhaps they're only a natural phenomenon. All people know for sure is that they form bridges to other worlds. They know this because off-world pilgrims come through every day in search of new lives.

But the portals only travel in one direction, and the trip is always one-way. It's a blind jump. A chance to start over.

"Next."

A middle-aged woman with salt-and-pepper hair steps forward, a stony, unreadable look on her face. The light swallows her whole.

Mark used to play it safe. There were too many uncertainties, he reasoned, too many unseen variables to gamble with excessive risk. So all his life he took the road most traveled. He graduated from college with a degree in accounting, because there was always demand for accountants. He got a comfortable desk job. He married. Bought a house. Had two children. Planned for retirement. He did everything by the book.

Then his wife and two children burned to death in an arson fire.

"Next."

A young man, hardly older than eighteen, steps forward. Light. Flash. Gone.

Mark planned for all the contingencies, and the universe compensated him with an absurd and senseless act of evil. He quit his job. Sold his house. Wandered the world in search of answers until his savings ran out.

Now, all that's left for him is to press forward into the unknown.

"Next."

Another man, this time well into his seventies. Another burst of indigo light and the man is gone.

Mark is now at the head of the line. This is it, he thinks. He's spent the last of his money on his ticket. Will life on the other side be better, or worse?

"Next."

The portal gate slides open. Mark steps forward and is embraced by the light.

Finding the Light

M ARY PEERED DOWN at the murky, gray-green water, pondering the cities and bodies that had slipped beneath its sallow, rippling surface during the night. All around her, a fetid wind whipped and whistled, mocking whispers in the faltering light.

"You failed," those voices seemed to say. "Before you even realized anything was wrong, you failed."

She looked up at the sun, low in the sky, bloated and red. It gave off a pale, sickly illumination that reminded her of congealed blood.

Just yesterday, the water had been a bright, electric blue; the sun, a blinding ball of white-hot fire. So much had changed. It was staggering to think how the corruption could have swept through the world so fast.

My ancestors defended it for tens of thousands of years, and I couldn't even defend it for one.

The wind became a dry, rasping laughter.

"The world has always been mine..." it seemed to say, and it sent its rotten, moldering stench to her nose, "since the time before time."

No, Mary couldn't accept that. Corruption had always been a part of the world—evil was an ever-present danger to be guarded against at all times—but there was also love, and this could not belong to evil any more than darkness could belong to the sun.

"I reject you," she said, stepping forward to the water's edge. "You hold no claim over these lands."

More laughter.

Mary held her ground.

"Dig deep," her father had told her once, his last lesson before taking up his mantle in the second life. "In times of distress, dig deep. Cling to what's right. Find the light and let it out into the world."

Dig deep.

Mary closed her eyes.

She reached far into Earth's heart, into the only place the corruption hadn't been able to touch. She could see that the light inside had faded, diminished by the relentless onslaught of the evil that forced it into hiding. But it was pure, strong, and true.

The Earth shuddered as Mary let out thick, gnarled roots. They surged through the ground, beneath soil and stone, down into the red-hot regions beneath, and plunged into the very core.

"What are you doing?" asked the wind, picking up in intensity, transforming into a hurricane-like gale.

With all the force she could muster, Mary pierced the white-hot center, making contact with the life force inside.

A bolt like an electric shock plowed through her, and shot up into the roots. With her as a conduit to lend it strength, it flowered into a radiance and a love so strong no corruption could survive its searing power. It flowed through her, out of her, out into the world.

"No!" cried that fetid wind, burning to cinders in the blinding luminescence. It boiled off like water, dispersing in a cloud of super-heated steam.

When at last she opened her eyes, the world was as she remembered it.

"You've done well," said the light, once more free to sustain the world.

Mary could no longer move, for her roots had run deep and there was no disentangling herself. She was one with Earth now, just as her father had been. And just as she would remain so for as long as the light allowed her to live.

"Take care of this world, so that I might always shine."

"I will," she whispered.

Now she gazed down at water that was a clear, crystal blue; the sun blazed overhead just as it had for thousands of years before. There would always be evil lurking in the shadows, but as long as there was light, redemption would be close at hand.

Going Home

Jack stood facing the Pacific, dwarfed by the immensity of the ocean. He was nothing before that endless expanse of blue. The vastness of the ocean made him ponder the vastness of the cosmos, transcendental, eternal. A tailwind kicked up behind him, billowing his shirt and jacket. He hugged himself and shivered.

He wanted to go home. He'd been away for too long, had almost forgotten what his other life was like. He'd married. Had kids. Grown old. He looked down at his hands, gnarled with age.

A wave rolled in, frothing at the edge. It reached as far as it could, grazed the surface of Jack's feet, then retreated, leaving behind a briny footprint.

His children were grown now and had families of their own. They hardly visited anymore. Would they miss him when he was gone? He supposed they might. He knew all too well that you never appreciated something until it was taken away.

No matter. They had all they needed to be self-sufficient. For a season they would mourn, and then they would go on to enjoy long, happy lives.

He peered at the sea with the rabid hunger of someone who hasn't eaten for months. The water called to him, sang his name in its maddening siren voice. The surf curled around his toes, tickling, teasing.

Jack had had enough of time. He would return to the sea, allow the water to take him, diffuse him, spread him around until he was as vast and timeless as it was. Someday he would emerge and venture back onto dry land—he thought the world might be very different by then, just as it had been on his last return—but he didn't want to think about that now.

He stepped forward, pulled his head back in ecstasy as the ocean embraced him like a prodigal son, and then he disappeared beneath the surface.

Gone

EVERYTHING WAS FINE, until he made a mistake.

It's gone now, the world—or at least the world he's always known. A subtle slip of the tongue, one mispronounced syllable, and the universe collapsed. So many lives, squeezed out of existence. Friends. Families. Cities. Nations. Gone.

He tries to undo the damage, to bring them all back. But every word moves the universe one step closer to ruin. At last he stops, too devastated and out of breath to continue. He stands alone in the dark, the world hazy and insubstantial.

He calls the words back, recants the damage wrought by his careless tongue. But once uttered, they will not return. The universe will not allow them.

He surveys the void and does not speak again.

Jeremy

J EREMY GLANCED DOWN at his hands, which were hidden beneath the table on his lap. A moment later, he closed his eyes. It was happening again.

Tiny beads of sweat appeared on his cheeks and forehead. He could feel the pressure mounting. He wouldn't be able to hold it in much longer.

"Please," he whispered. "Not again."

He looked around the crowded downtown plaza and panicked.

He saw a familiar-looking man bite into a sandwich, and his mind made a jump cut to his old best friend Patrick, who'd disappeared when he was only ten. He turned and spotted a pair of brightly dressed women chatting at a table, and was instantly transported back to high school, to the girls he'd always wanted to talk to but never had the courage to approach. They, too, had disappeared.

"Why is this happening?" Jeremy asked, grasping the table with trembling, white-knuckled hands. He could feel the power welling up inside, knew that it would burst from him like fireworks no matter what he did.

He looked down at his hands again. They'd begun to glow a faint, swampy green.

"Not again," he moaned. "Please, not again."

He clamped down harder on the table. His grip was so tight he thought it might snap in two. Then he convulsed. His head whipped back, his stomach clenched, and he was certain everything he'd eaten for a year would come back up again. He gasped and shuddered. Shrieked. Brightness filled his vision.

A moment later, all was dark.

T HE FIRST LIGHT to reach Jeremy's eyes was cracked and broken, a kaleidescope of disjoint shapes. He lifted his head mechanically and sat up straight.

When his mind came back online, he whirled around. He searched his surroundings, already knowing what he would find, but hoping this time would be different.

Jeremy was alone.

The tables were empty. There was no sign anyone had ever been there. Silence hovered over the plaza like a thick fog. Tears began to fall from Jeremy's eyes. He raked a hand through his hair, gazed up at the sky and shouted.

"Why?"

It was the same thing that had happened to Patrick and the girls from high school. They were there. Then his hands started to glow. There was light, then dark; when he came to, they were gone.

The glow was gone now, just as it had gone before. Now, all he could do was wonder how long it would be before it happened again.

Journey's End

IT WAS BIG. World-sized big. It towered over her, blocking her path. So, this was what her journey had come to. Centuries of trudging through deserts and mountains, seas and jungles, space and time, only so minutes from her journey's end, a stone wall could block her path. It shot up into the sky and beyond; it extended to the left and right as far as the eye could see.

She fell to the dusty ground, bowed her head, and cried.

She could remember when she'd first set out, how young and beautiful she'd been, so full of ambition and drive. She cleaved to her mission with an almost childlike devotion. Then she aged. Her features weathered, until she was like many of the deserts she'd passed through on the way. Youthful optimism yielded first to caution, then to exhaustion. In the end, only gritty persistence and determination saw her come so close to the other side.

She'd faced many obstacles, pushed through quite a few toils, trials, and dangers. There were times when she was convinced she couldn't go on, when she thought in long bouts of despair that she might as well lay down to die, letting her bleached bones adorn her path, serving as a warning to others who might dare follow in her footsteps.

Then she reconsidered, thinking that perhaps she should encourage rather than frighten her fellow explorers. After all, more were setting out every day for the same reason she had, to be a part of something bigger, something transcendent and everlasting. So instead, she let her struggle bear witness to the fact that anything was possible, that if you wanted something badly enough, you could seize it by sheer willpower alone.

And that's all this was, she realized, another obstacle, one more test before she could finally indulge in the fruit of her labor. She only had to be strong and pick herself up from the ground one last time.

She rose and beat the dust off of her shirt, pants, and boots. Wiped away her tears. She stared at the rock face before her, until a grim smile pushed past her own ancient features.

"Okay," she said to the wall. "Let's do this."

She launched herself at it, pried, picked, and climbed for as long as she could. But the hard granite surface was unyielding. It dug into her skin, scratching, tearing.

Then, just when she'd offered all her strength, when she felt she had no blood left to shed, a harsh baritone rumble swallowed the world. The wall moved down, sucked into the Earth. She watched, mesmerized, until first the sky, then the mountains beyond became visible. An entire vista opened before her eyes, a glittering otherworldly refuge of gold, silver, and crystal. It was the most beautiful thing she had ever seen.

When the last of the wall had disappeared beneath the ground, she stepped forward. She'd done it. She was on the other side.

Labyrinth

A THICK FOG, billowing like smoke, surrounded Gerald. The world beyond the Labyrinth lay bare before him, pale and insubstantial, faded like an old photograph. He'd navigated the Labyrinth's perilous depths for centuries, a towering ancient structure of stone, iron, and magic. All the while, he'd labored under the promise that someday, when he'd reached the end, he would be released.

Now he knew the truth.

He could see the world outside, only it was a mute shadow of the place he'd known before he was captured. It would be forever out of reach.

His conquerors had said the Labyrinth was a Purgatory, that at the end he would find pardon and peace. But the Labyrinth was not a Purgatory, it was a Hell. Its purpose had not been to redeem him but to break him.

Head hung low, shoulders hunched in defeat, he turned to go back the way he'd come.

Life in Reverse

IT WAS HAPPENING AGAIN. A cosmic hiccup. A moment in time, repeated. The world moved around her, but in reverse. How many times had Stacy been through the same series of events? She might have been through a single iteration, or she might have been through a thousand. Forward. Then backward.

Water rose from the shag carpet like liquid crystal, streamed back into a glass that reflected sharp needles of light as it fell upward, arcing through the air and finally righting itself on Mary Anne's serving tray. The woman back-stepped from pale and mortified to warm and boisterous.

In an insane corner of her mind, the part of her that was convinced she'd done this long enough for the sun to burn out, Stacy wondered if God had found some particular event in the world so funny that he'd had to hit the rewind button to watch it again.

Then she wondered if this was Hell.

Mark's shoulder disconnected from Mary Anne's, just as his foot parted ways from the table leg that had tripped him. His head came up like an Olympic swimmer rising from the water. All of this in a world without sound.

How could that be? Shouldn't she hear everything, but backward? Did it have to do with waves of sound traveling backward instead of forward, toward instead of away from the source? Maybe, though she suspected that wasn't quite right.

During all of this, she was frozen, like the ice sculpture mounted beside the chocolate fountain, dripping backward as it spontaneously refroze. Like the T-1000 in the second Terminator movie, she thought. A mad giggle would have escaped her lips if she could have opened them.

Lucy stepped back into her field of vision, approached her in a strange backward walk as she un-dismissed herself from Stacy's company. She had no idea how far back time would go before things righted themselves, but a sense of certainty was mounting that the stage was nearly set for the next iteration.

She thought of the movie *Groundhog Day*. Was there a lesson in this? If so, why couldn't she remember any of her previous experiences? She suspected, much to her horror, that this was pure accident, that the universe wasn't so neat and orderly after all. That, more than anything else, scared her.

If this was immortality, she wanted to die.

Lucy's mouth opened. The arm she'd withdrawn from Stacy's shoulder returned. And that was when she felt it, a tug, an instant of hopeless disorientation as the universe stopped, tilted, began to spin in the opposite direction once more. In one infinitesimal moment, she felt she was on the precipice of something, that she existed outside space and time, that she was nearly a god. Then memory drained from her head like water down a drain.

"Stacy," said Lucy, a hand on her shoulder. "It was so good of you to come. Let me see if I can find Steve so he can say hello." She left Stacy and searched her boyfriend.

Then there was a shocked cry, a mortified apology, and the dull thud of a glass landing on the carpet. Stacy's eyes went to the wet spot, and she could swear that just beyond that darkened halo of shag carpet there was some cosmic secret, a hidden trap that was about to spring.

Another tug, then a pull. The muscles in Stacy's body froze, and a knowledge that wasn't quite memory returned to her. It was happening again.

A moment in time, repeated.

Love Between the Lines

HE BEGINS TO WAKE.
The dream warps, fades, falls away to the space between. On the periphery of his subconscious, just before the threshold of reality, is where he meets Diane.

He can feel himself slipping; he feels the world around him breaking apart like dandelion fluff in a breeze, and it's in this moment that she caresses him against her breast. He cannot see her, and he dares not open his eyes for fear of shattering the fragile state in which he enjoys her divine company.

He wills the encounter to last—wills the future to melt like the wax of a brightly burning candle to reveal a single ever-present moment. But sooner or later, the bubble will pop, and he knows that when it does he'll be left alone in the dark, awake, heartbroken, aching for the next time their worlds intersect.

There is no lasting peace for him, no enduring joy. There is only Diane and their love between the lines.

Mirage

Richelle wandered up and down Sunset Boulevard, purse swinging by her side, holding up a hand every so often to shield her eyes from the afternoon sun. Everything seemed perfectly ordinary, and yet...

Something wasn't right. There was nothing wrong with her surroundings as far as she could tell, nothing wrong with herself. But at the same time, *everything* was wrong.

A shimmer caught Richelle's eye and she turned.

A towering skyscraper stood to the west, gleaming beneath the sun like a world-sized diamond. It snagged her gaze and refused to let go. As she stared, something inside of her snapped into focus.

She had to get to that building.

She was walking faster now, high heels clip-clopping like horseshoes on the hot cement. People continued about their business, yet she thought she caught strangers eyeing her askance. She could hear voices now, as if from far away—a low, vibrating hum almost too low for her to hear.

What were they saying? She thought if she listened carefully...

Someone bumped into her, knocked her to the ground.

"Sorry, lady," said a man in a white polo. "Didn't see you." But somewhere beneath his voice, she thought she'd heard another say, "It's her!"

Rattled, she picked herself up, stammered, "That's—that's all right," and brushed past him.

In the distance, that crystalline edifice called to her, shimmering like a mirage. Only she thought that wasn't quite right.

The world is the mirage. That building is the only real thing here.

The thought was shattering in its clarity. There came another.

I have to get to that building.

But no sooner did she continue walking than another man in a white polo bumped into her.

"Pardon me," he said, scurrying off. And somewhere beyond, in another layer of reality, she heard: "Stop her!"

Reeling now, Richelle broke into a sprint.

Have to get to that building!

Smack. Another man in a white polo.

"So sorry!"

Smack. Another man in a white polo.

"Excuse me."

Smack.

Smack.

Smack.

Richelle was surrounded now, drowning in an ocean of men in white polos. Her breaths came in increasingly shallow gasps.

What is this?

All around her, beyond the absent-minded apologies, clamored a chorus of darker voices.

"Can't allow her to reach the building."

"Can't you see her?"

"She's over there."

"Stop her!"

They were not men, she decided, nor was this a real city. Moreover, they knew she knew and they were trying to keep her from discovering the truth.

Richelle was angry now.

Planting her feet to the ground, she hefted her purse in both hands and swung it in a wide arc.

It whistled through the air before smashing into a target.

"Ouch! What'd you do that for?" The man clutched his bleeding nose and stared at her as if she'd gone insane. Beneath his voice was another: "Kill her!"

The ocean of bodies pressed tighter, became a swarm of flesh-eating flies. All the while, she swung her purse and slowly pushed on, inching her way toward the building.

She couldn't remember how long she'd been fighting, but, when she looked up again, the sun was a bloated red ball hovering close to the horizon, and directly before her was the building, only yards away now, a wildfire of reflected light that seared her retinas whenever she looked directly at it.

Richelle screamed, a feral cry that seemed to resonate with the city and its malicious inhabitants. The men clutched at their ears as if enduring an unbearable agony, and Richelle continued shrieking until her lungs were depleted and her throat was raw.

When she could no longer sustain the sound, she made a beeline for those last few yards, ignoring the arms that reached for her, trying to grab at her clothing and hair, trying to pull her back into the crowd.

Richelle stopped just short of that magnificent structure and was suddenly dwarfed by its size. She squinted up at the fiery light reflected from its surface. For a moment, it seemed to capture a different light and scatter it across the city in an otherworldly spectrum.

On the surface, it appeared transparent and made of glass, yet it was opaque to her in some way she didn't understand. Her eyes fixed on a simple door set into the foundation, the only part of it she could see clearly.

"Stop her!" those voices commanded again, but it was too late. Her hand was already on the door.

She turned. Pulled.
The door opened.

Picking Up the Pieces

S HE LIVES AT THE CROSSROADS of time and space. The rest of her kind left long ago, choosing to search for a new world instead of trying to repair the one they already had. But she couldn't go with them. This was her homeland, the world that had given birth to her. She couldn't let it die. Now she stands alone in a barren land, trying to pick up the pieces they left behind.

Trying to rebuild.

She dreams of how things were, focuses her power on reversing the decay. She grits her teeth as that power flows out of her, and she picks the constituent pieces of her reality off the ground and molds them into something new.

It is slow, lonely work.

Her world was vast, and the universe will nearly be in its death throes by the time she's finished. But she hopes that if she fixes it, they will return. Without them, without her world as it once was, she knows she'll never be whole.

Precious Stones

Ainsley plunged his hands into the icy water. He scraped the ground beneath until they were filled with stones and pulled them back above the surface. He examined each pebble, cursed when he didn't find what he was looking for, and chucked the entire load back into the water.

Behind him, the rocky shore rattled like a string of beads as the tide pulled out.

The beach here was composed wholly of stones of all shapes, sizes, and colors. Once, when the world was new, they'd all been a dazzling white, each saturated with the wild, unformed magic of creation. But most had surrendered their magic eons ago, had used their nearly limitless power to manufacture the world. Now, the majority were worthless trinkets.

The majority, but not all.

Ainsley reeled in another handful. Examined it. Tossed it back and tried again.

There were a few albinos left, cosmic leftovers scattered like flecks of diamond in the sand of a desert. Those precious few were still filled with the raw power of creation, a magic orders of magnitude stronger than anything magicians could wield today.

The water was cold, and Ainsley shivered.

Once he'd thought he could avoid the ocean, that he could restrict his search to the rocks he saw on the shore. After all, he'd reasoned, it was equally likely that he'd discover an albino on land as he would in the water. But further research in the dustier corners of the Archives had indicated this was not the case, that searching outside the sea would have been a waste of time. The type of object he sought was drawn to the water like a magnet was drawn to iron. So he continued to sift the shallow ocean floor, cold and tired and alone.

A shuddering gasp as he mined the bottom again. More worthless rocks. They plopped back into the water with all the rest.

The beach where Ainsley had spent his life searching was a special place, hidden in a forgotten corner of the world where few ventured and from which fewer returned. It had taken him ages to find it, and his search for even a single stone had consumed double that amount of time.

Long ago, he'd been an influential magician himself. He'd fundamentally changed theory as well as its application with his groundbreaking research. For a time, he'd even served as one of the Tower's Council of Nine. But then his research had led him down an unorthodox path, and before he knew what had happened, he'd been exiled by his colleagues, who were convinced he'd made a mockery of their field. The day they sent him away, they called him a lunatic. But he knew better, and he would prove them wrong.

More rocks. Worthless. Dump. Repeat.

He was tired, had turned into a feeble old man while his back was turned, and from time to time he worried he'd die a failure, that his life's work would be in vain. The years he'd traveled back and forth between the layers of the world to get to this place had taken their toll, and though he was only forty-seven, he looked and felt like a man of eighty.

He closed his eyes. Scooped up more rocks. Opened his eyes. Looked down. Gray and orange, red and black, but no white. He tossed them one by one, watched as they landed with tiny as well as not so tiny ripples.

Then he stopped. There, tucked beneath a larger stone in the palm of his hand, a tiny white pebble. His breath caught in his throat. He picked it up with his other hand, let the rest fall back into the water, forgotten. This was what he'd spent his life searching for.

In that single pebble was more energy than a thousand men could wield in a lifetime. The power to level mountains. The power to raise new ones. He could feel it humming just beneath the surface like a high-tension electrical wire.

A smile bloomed on the man's salt-parched lips as he thought of his former colleagues. Wouldn't they be surprised...

Selina

THE OLD MAN hunched over an antique desk beneath the dim light of a small lamp. An open notebook stared up at him, empty though he'd been sitting there for hours.

Once, when he was young, he'd enjoyed a vibrant career. Back then, the words had flowed like wine. He'd brought stories into the world the likes of which had never been told before. But now in his old age, the well had run dry.

Of course, his books had never been his own. That was his dirty secret, the thing he kept from his readers whenever they asked him where he got his ideas. He'd always offer the standard bullshit, that he'd been a reclusive child, that it was his retreat into fiction that changed the way he saw and thought about the world.

But the truth was, he was a fraud, for while the writing had been his own, the stories had come from someone else.

When he was only a teenager, a visitor came to him during the night. A woman, garbed in flowing silk that glowed in the dark.

"Wake up," she whispered.

He almost screamed when he saw her, but she placed a hand over his mouth and assured him she meant no harm. She said her name was Selina, that she'd wandered the world in search of someone to tell her story. She placed a finger to her lips. Then she covered his eyes.

What followed was a supernova of sights and sounds, streaming before his eyes like a cosmic newsreel. An excerpt from a life outside the universe.

When he finally came back to himself, she was gone.

A notebook and pen had been left beside him. An open invitation, he thought, and he stayed up until dawn, trying to capture some small part of what he'd glimpsed in the mysterious vision.

She came to him the following night, and the night after that. Each time, he would sit down after she'd left to search out words that might do justice to the otherworldly snapshots of her life.

The books that resulted propelled him to unheard of heights. Nobody had read anything like these stories. People fawned over his work. Even the sharpest critics seemed to be at a loss.

But five years ago, Selina stopped visiting.

He flailed, struggled to recall something of her supernal sojourn through the stars. But without those visions to guide his work, his writing became derivative, stale, and uninteresting. People stopped buying his books. Eventually, he locked himself inside his house and never went out again.

Now, he gazed up at the lamp, still at a loss after five years. He closed his eyes, and he wondered if Selina would ever visit again.

Shattered Reality

Déjà vu. Everything is the same as it was before.

Jordan sees her by the register, standing in line with a gallon of milk and a plastic bag of carrots. She looks so much like the woman he's been searching for, the woman he loved for many years—his wife, the mother of his child. He wants to run to her, to embrace her, to tell her they can be a family again. But before he can move, he knows it isn't her.

She looks the same. She has the same dark brown hair, the same olive skin, the same heart-shaped face. He knows that if he approaches her, she'll grab her ear and smile in the same self-conscious way that won him over so early on in their relationship. It's Karen, but it isn't *his* Karen.

He was foolish to toy with something as brittle as space and time. He breached the barrier between the worlds, and the universe shattered, torn into a billion partial reflections of his own reality. He was flung clear of the blast, soared headlong into a cosmos that was not his own, and now he must find his way home.

For a moment, just like every other moment since the accident, he considers that this world is good enough.

He reaches for her. Puts his arm down. Reaches for her again. Finally, he hangs his head. This is not his home, not his Karen. She'll have chosen another Jordan, and they'll have had another baby Angelina.

Not his home. Not his wife. Jordan turns away.

He opens the palm of his hand, raises it toward the ceiling, and a gateway appears, a hole in space that only he can see. He marches forward, resigned, and is consumed by gray.

Maybe the next world will be his own.

Showdown

FEAR. It surrounds me.

I awoke this morning to discover that dangers and perils of every kind had gathered around me during the night, intent on doing me harm. I look each in the eye. I swallow.

A showdown.

How did this happen? I cast my mind to the distant past, try to pinpoint the exact moment the trajectory of my life turned in this direction. I fail.

I shut my eyes against the inevitable. "Take me," I whisper. "I won't be afraid anymore."

I wait.

Slowly I open my eyes. They haven't gone, but neither have they moved. This time, I thrust my chest out more boldly. "I said, take me!" I cry into the morning, naked and vulnerable, daring them to attack. "Do what you came to do."

Silence.

I begin to shake, not with fear but with adrenaline. A giddy absurdity overtakes me, and the enemies that stand before me are transfigured. Weapons, armor, and bared teeth become plastic toys, children's costumes, and toothless gums, flailing before me in a parody of force.

I learn the truth.

My enemies, who had been so strong in their denouncements, who had whispered of my destruction in the middle of the night, who had vowed to tear me limb from limb the instant I ventured into the world they'd been guarding so jealously; they had only ever been harmless specters, useless projections sent to prevent me from taking what had always rightfully been mine.

I stand.

I look at my aggressors, impotent and without life. I step forward. They shout at me through silent lips, brandishing their plastic pitchforks and red-capped toy pistols. I laugh. The sound is a deep, earthy rumble. It consumes me, makes me whole.

The specters disappear.

I am reborn.

The Book

THERE IS A BOOK. It is written not in English or Spanish, Greek or Latin, Hebrew or Arabic, but in the wordless language of Creation. It is a series of divine utterances, a wellspring of stars, energy, and life.

Once, it was passed from one keeper to the next, an unbroken succession rooted in merit rather than blood or prestige. It was a cosmic secret to be guarded, and it was never to be opened. But thousands of years ago, the last keeper tried to violate this rule. He was slain, and the book went missing. Those who remembered it had children and grandchildren, then died. The book passed from memory to legend, and from legend it was forgotten.

Like an ocean swell, civilizations rose, civilizations fell. All the while, the book hid beyond the shadows, watching, waiting for its next keeper—someone worthy of its secrets, someone who would at last be allowed to open its dusty weather-worn pages, for it so longed to be read.

Now, it sits upon a humble library shelf.

Today it spies Garrett, a child of ten years, who happens to be at the very same library. The book gazes down at him, peers into his soul, sees that he is worthy. It drops from the shelf into the boy's backpack, and the boy, unknowing, carries it home with him. He does his homework. Watches TV. Eats dinner. Prepares for bed.

Meanwhile, the book finds its way onto Garrett's mattress, and there it waits beneath the covers.

After Garrett climbs into bed, after the winds of sleep have begun to carry him away to secret lands, the book nudges his shoulder.

Garrett wakes.

Half asleep, he reaches out, taps the ancient leather spine with his fingers.

He opens his eyes. Fully awake, he rises to a sitting position, reaches into the sheets and pulls the book out into the open. *Where did this come from*, he wonders. He opens it. A warm light shines on his face.

Garrett flips through empty, weathered pages, and a universe springs to life.

The Edge of the World

HE WAS NINE the year he lost his grandfather. All that was left was a note: "Gone to the edge of the world." He never saw him again. At age seventy-five, the man decided to follow in his grandfather's footsteps.

His grandfather would tell him stories about the edge of the world, how his own father had taken him to see it when he was only a child, how they'd sailed across the ocean for months on a private boat, how the experience had haunted him the rest of his life. He'd said that with every passing year, it called to him with increasing urgency, until it was all he could do to keep from running away and jumping into the empty cosmos beyond.

He used to think they were just stories. Now he knew better.

He was an educated man, and he knew the world was round. He'd flown all over the globe, had explored more than a dozen countries in pursuit of something elusive and unseen, something that up until very recently had remained an unarticulated mystery. He also knew that if you sailed long enough, you'd encounter the edge of the world. He was certain because he'd been there.

He'd sold everything he owned, bought a small boat, and sailed for months without stopping, just as his grandfather had told him he had. It wasn't hard to find. He only had to choose the brightest star in the sky and follow it across the horizon.

The journey was long and perilous, and after he ran out of food and water, he was sure death would take him.

That was when he found what he was looking for.

Most people, if they believe in the edge of the world, think it's somewhere in the middle of the ocean, a colossal waterfall cascading down into endless black. His grandfather had known better, and the old man had passed the knowledge on to him.

His tiny boat washed up on an impossibly large shore, a flat carpet of wind-smoothed sand. He blinked when he came to a stop, hardly daring to believe he'd been successful. He tumbled awkwardly over the side, pushed himself to his feet, and reached back into the boat to pull out an old gas-lit lantern. He removed a set of matches from his pocket, which he'd carefully packed inside multiple layers of plastic bags to keep them dry, and ignited the burner to produce a flickering flame. Finally, lantern at the forefront, he pressed into the dark, the flame forming a small orange halo on the sand.

His grandfather had told him this place was special, that here it was always night, and what he found corroborated the old man's story. Though his watch said it was two-thirty in the afternoon, the cosmos was laid bare before him, naked and unashamed, stars dusting the sky like ground gemstones. And ahead, just a few hundred meters away, was the edge of the world.

It was not the steep drop of a precipice. Instead, the sand, turned pale gray in the light of the moon, faded to black like a fine mist, pocked occasionally by tiny wellsprings of darkness like miniature black holes. As he walked, the ground became mushy, soft, and pliable. And ahead, where he dared not go, it thinned to a nearly transparent film, beneath which there was only the black of space and the shimmering stars beyond.

He lifted his head and the lantern, risked a peek over the edge. But the space beyond swallowed the feeble light and refused to reflect any of it back. Well, he supposed there were some mysteries that weren't meant to be solved, at least not on this side of the cosmic divide.

Anyway, he would discover soon enough what the universe was keeping from him. It had been calling to him for a while, only he hadn't recognized the call for what it was. Until now.

He stood at the edge and gazed into eternal night. "I'm coming, grandfather."

Then he closed his eyes and jumped.

The Forgotten Magic

THE MAN STOOD beneath the moon and the stars, desperate and afraid. The world was bearing down on him, threatening to crush him under its immense and unyielding weight. He leaped into the air uselessly, tried in vain to spread his arms and fly.

Long ago, on the outer periphery of time and memory, he could have done it—could have sprouted wings, kicked the dust from his feet, and soared into the air. But that power was lost to him now, forgotten with age and responsibility.

He couldn't go on. He no longer had the energy to trudge through the trenches of daily life. He needed to escape, to run far away from the world and its heartless machinations.

He leaped again, flapping his arms from side to side like an off-balance windmill. It was useless. The man nearly cried.

When had the world lost its magic? When had it transformed from a bright glowing ball of potential energy to a soulless machine that had consumed his humanity and left nothing of it for him? He had given the world everything, and the world had spared nothing for him in return.

The man looked up, away from the world. He gazed at the stars, and they gazed back at him with ancient understanding. If only he could touch them. They seemed to call his name, and he was certain that all he had to do was answer.

Had he changed? Was that why he'd forgotten? Perhaps the world had always been what it was. Perhaps the problem was not that the world had changed, but that he himself had changed. Perhaps the magic was not gone after all. Perhaps it had only been neglected, a childhood toy abandoned in an attic.

He basked in the light of the moon, bathed in it until he felt pure. Finally, he donned the cosmos like a cloak. The stars accepted him then, adopted him as their son. In a flash of clarity, they granted him the gift of memory.

He let it all go. He laid his burdens before the stars as a sacrifice, an offering to be exchanged for something much older, something pristine, something everlasting. He closed his eyes and the magic overtook him.

Transformed into something both new and ancient, he spread his arms, which turned into the wings of an eagle. He flapped, and he could feel the air push back against him, countering gravity, bearing him high into the atmosphere. He flew toward the stars.

He didn't look back and he never returned.

The Game

L IFE SURROUNDS ME. Thousands of spectators, crammed into seats on risers stacked ten stories high, encircling a field of green where two teams engage in a sport the humans call baseball. A player swings a heavy wooden bat, which smacks into a tiny white ball, producing a loud crack. The ball sails somewhere into the third level. The crowd cheers.

Seated on the second level, I watch it pass overhead and smile.

I can feel the heat of living blood, throbbing all around me like sonorous drums. With a crowd this large, I can do anything.

Some people think the greatest magic lies in words, that if they recite a certain combination of sounds a certain number of times, they'll compel the cosmos to give up its secrets. But words are weak, crude expressions whose meanings invariably drift with time. Magicians skilled in the art of spelling might amass small scraps of power, but their deeds rarely amount to more than parlor tricks.

Life, on the other hand, is a great, untapped reservoir, a fount of limitless energies. One must only possess the secret of its use, and in all my thousands of years, I can count such knowledge among my achievements.

I send out tiny tendrils, like runners from a creeping vine, and probe my closest neighbors. When they make contact, a warm power flows into me. Ecstasy. I'm careful not to draw too much at once, feeding only on the surplus energies that this game has so conveniently produced. Then, using my neighbors as proxies, I send out more tendrils, until they're slithering through the stadium like snakes, harvesting energy in a vast, intricate network that feeds back to me.

The people cheer once more. This time, a wave of power washes over me. I bask in its brilliance. I channel it, weave the individual flows until they form a rope-like column that towers toward the sky.

What I accomplish today will fundamentally and irrevocably change the world. I lick my lips, savor the captivating notion of a world on the brink.

I close my eyes and unleash my magic.

The Gift

THE MAN SAT on a long wooden bench, watching a little boy no older than two play in the grass. He saw him kick a soft blue ball and thought the sight should have made him smile. But he only felt despair, an aching emptiness that had hardened his heart long ago. He'd lived a long life, had expected so much and received so little. He had no spouse, no family, no friends. He'd spent the better part of his days drifting from one thing to the next, always in pursuit of something better, a dream only half-glimpsed, always on the edge of the horizon and forever out of reach. Now his life was like his eyes, blurred and unfocused in his old age.

The boy chased after his soft, blue ball. When he caught up with it, he laughed, drew back his right leg, and kicked. The ball rolled along the dewy grass, cut across the asphalt path, and skittered to a stop just below the man's worn brown shoes. He looked down at the boy, and he tried so very hard to smile. Instead he sighed, gave the ball a light kick, and watched as the boy took off after it.

The boy picked up his ball. Returned to the man. Eyed him curiously and smiled.

The man said, "Hi." He tried to make his voice light and playful. He succeeded only in a tone that was dull and flat.

The boy frowned and came closer, cradling the ball in his arms. He peered into the man's eyes, tilting his head slightly, and extended his arms outward, gesturing with his soft, blue ball.

"Ball?" The boy dropped the toy into the man's lap.

His eyes brimmed with unexpected tears. "For me?" he asked, pointing to himself with a finger that trembled only partially due to old joints.

The boy smiled in reply.

Such kindness. For what seemed the first time in a very long life, the man cracked a smile, thin and awkward as it was. The boy had given him a gift greater than anything he'd ever received. A tiny spark that had lain dormant in the man's heart for many years ignited, and he let the awkward smile bloom into a broad grin.

The boy saw the change in the man's face and giggled.

That was when he realized he, too, had a gift to give—a gift he'd almost forgotten, a gift he'd never expected to give himself.

"For your kindness," the man said, "I give the oldest gift, the oldest and the greatest."

He extended his right hand, laid it atop the boy's head. A sudden gust of wind scattered strands of the boy's light-blond hair.

The man closed his eyes and turned his gaze inward. He peered into the boy's heart, examined the boy's future. He saw all that the boy was and all that he would become.

"You will hold this gift in your heart always. I pray that you treasure it and that you never let it die. Most of all, I pray that you'll have the opportunity to share it with another."

The boy frowned, comprehending nothing. No matter. Knowledge would come when the boy was ready. Knowing was its own gift, one that gave itself in its own time, one that could be accepted or rejected when the boy came of age.

The man muttered a string of words he'd once thought himself incapable of articulating, and for a brief moment the space between the boy's head and the man's hand seemed to glow, a brilliant gold that highlighted the boy's blond hair. A moment later, the light died and the man opened his eyes.

The man said, "Go." He spoke gently, smiled warmly.

The boy took his ball and ran, bobbing awkwardly as he kept the toy clutched against his chest.

The man exhaled deeply, content. Finally, he'd given what he himself had received so many decades ago, a light he'd turned away from when he was a young man. He hoped the boy would pass it on. He was strong, and the man had seen great things in his future.

His life's work, he now realized, was complete. He'd done what he came into the world to do, and now it was time to go home. His eyelids grew heavy and began to fall. His breathing slowed, and he fell into a permanent, dreamless sleep.

He was free now, and he would never be unhappy again.

The Machine

I F YOU LISTEN CAREFULLY, you can hear it, the low, bass rumble of hulking iron gears winding behind a cosmic curtain, beyond space and time. It sustains the universe, scaffolds reality. Once, when the machine was new, when it was well oiled and regularly maintained, it made little sound at all, just a gentle soothing hum that saturated the universe with nascent energy.

But gradually, almost imperceptibly, the steady, nearly silent rhythm began to change. At first, it was just a tiny ping in the engine. Then the oil began to burn and the gears began to grind. Yet the machine continued to operate to specification, and the universe chugged along for another fourteen billion years.

Then the ball bearings gave out. The machine started to crack and squeak, and the universe began to spoil. Stars began to lose their heat. Gravity began to lose its pull. Time warped and stretched like taffy. All the while, that incessant squealing permeated the cosmos, driving men, women, and beings of indeterminate gender mad.

Finally, the timing belt snapped and the whole thing unraveled. There was a crash, a thud, and the machine simply stopped running. Reality wavered. Faded. Disappeared.

For ages, the machine sat in disrepair, silent and still, ruined and forgotten in the darkness outside creation. Then its maker stumbled onto it while seeking parts for another project. He considered leaving it, for he was a busy man. But nostalgia seized him, and he was overtaken by an unexpected sadness.

He toiled in endless dark. He replaced the timing belt and the ball bearings. He lubricated the sensitive inner workings. He filled the reservoir with a fresh carton of oil.

When at last he was finished, he flipped the switch. The machine spun to life, and the universe was new once more. And in the background, permeating space and time, was that familiar, ever-present hum.

The Music Within

THE MUSIC CALLED TO STEVE, and he skipped work early to follow after it.

He rushed home, head down, on his way back to his apartment. All the while, that spectral, otherworldly tune twined through him, shooting feelers into his heart, penetrating the darkest corners of his soul. He bolted up the stairs, dug through his pockets for his key, opened the door, and slipped inside.

The room was dark, with only a sliver of late-afternoon sun seeping through the shuttered window. But he didn't turn on the light. Instead, he sat beside the coffee table where his violin lay, the polished surface catching the minuscule light from the window so that it seemed to glow.

He took the instrument into his hands, and the music within swirled, coalesced. He ran a finger along the smooth, wood-grain surface. An electric charge surged down his spine. The music was pounding at his skull now, demanding to have its way with him, and he was ready to oblige.

It was going to sweep him away, he thought, carry him to that other world once more—a world where music was the language of creation, a world under siege, a world that needed his help if it was going to survive. He was afraid, but the music had embraced him like a lover, and Steve was powerless to resist.

He held the bow above the strings. Paused. Sighed.

He began to play.

This has been turned into a novella called Swept Away.

The Traveler

ROB LAY DOWN and closed his eyes. It was time to sleep.

Darkness. Relaxation. A moment in eternity, suspended in the half-life of semi-consciousness. Then he was drifting away from the waking world.

He was a traveler, an empyreal wanderer who roamed the spaces not accessible to him during his waking hours. He didn't know if there were others like him, didn't know if his talent was common or rare, only that it was fundamental to his nature.

There was a doorway in the distance, a bridge between Earth and the infinite expanse beyond. Rob rushed toward it eagerly, trailed by the ephemeral white mist that connected him to the slumbering body back at his apartment. It opened as he approached, and he stopped for a moment on the threshold to marvel at the celestial canvas beyond, universes stacked on universes, a cosmos of limitless bounds.

He took it in, a deep breath of the freshest spiritual air, then he burst through the doorway like a rocket. He soared through the stars, a soul unfettered by the shackles of solid form. He could be anybody, anything. He thought of a bird, and he was flapping his wings in an endless expanse of blue. He thought of an ocean, and he was feeling his immense world-sized body crash into the rocks. In a timeless instant that could have been a millisecond or a thousand years, he cycled through an uncountable array of creatures and structures, physical and abstract, visited an unknowable number of worlds, alien and familiar.

Then, suddenly, there was a presence. It bubbled up around him, cutting off his flight. It reached for him with oily, tainted feelers. Rob recoiled. He'd never seen anything like it, had never been afraid in this place before today. He dashed back toward the doorway between the worlds.

It followed. He could feel it gaining on him. If he stayed, he thought it might sever the cord that connected him to Earth, that it would carry him away to someplace dark and cold.

Almost there. He was almost back on the other side. But just as he'd started to wake, that dark entity snatched him from behind. He could feel the mattress beneath his head, feel his lungs rise and fall as his body breathed, yet he couldn't move his arms or legs, couldn't open his eyes. The world was still black, with that dark presence trying to reel him in.

He tried to kick loose, but its grip wouldn't budge. Meanwhile, the heart back in his body started to race, the lungs drawing in shorter and shallower breaths. He lunged at his body, scrambled to reanimate muscles that had been frozen by the paralysis of sleep. But it was maddeningly out of reach. All the while, that mysterious entity continued to pull, dragging him inch by inch.

Rob clawed, scratched, dug in tight with his heels. Finally its hold began to slip. He could feel himself slide closer to his body. Reach. He had to reach. Just a bit farther. He could almost move a finger. The entity yanked harder, but Rob gave it everything he had. Finally the muscles in his fingers twitched. He felt the doorway between the two worlds begin to close behind him. He was almost there. Almost—

The door slammed shut.

Rob bolted from the mattress in a pall of cold sweat, heart thundering in his chest. He scrambled to catch his breath. He'd made it, but barely. What was that thing? Was he safe now?

For the first time in his life, Rob was afraid to go back to sleep.

The World Fire

D APPLED LIGHT DANCED across Vivian's face, a hypnotic electric blue. She'd traveled long and far to get here, to the ends of the Earth and back. So much pain. So much loss. Time had passed her by as she wandered the darker passages of the world, until everyone and everything she'd ever known was dead.

"The World Fire accepts your sacrifice," said the priestess sitting cross-legged opposite the brightest flames Vivian had ever seen, an azure blaze that sizzled and popped with raw, untamable energy. "Come and accept your gift."

Vivian shambled forward, a painful lump bulging in her throat as she swallowed. She hadn't eaten in three days and she was weak. When at last, after God knew how many centuries of wandering, she'd finally arrived at the underground temple's gates, she'd expected the answers she sought to be laid before her feet. Instead, the priestesses had denied her entry, requiring her first to fast.

"Please," she'd said, weary and starving. But they'd been adamant, and Vivian had been put up in a tiny monastic cell outside the temple proper with no source of light, save for the dim flicker of an oil lamp, the flame blue, like all the fire down there.

"Do you know why we made you fast?" the priestess asked, her face shrouded by a dark cloth.

Vivian shook her head. She was muzzy and couldn't think straight. She'd tried to meet the priestess's eyes, but the fire kept drawing her attention, wild energies she'd lusted for her entire life.

"The World Fire demands sacrifice," the woman said in a low voice. "Even after all you gave up in search of it, you were required to give up more, because only with your stomach and your heart empty can you partake of its secrets."

Vivian licked her lips. There were many theories pertaining to what the fire was and what it could do, ranging from the plausible to the fantastical and everything in between. She hadn't known what to expect when she set out, then a young woman disillusioned with life, but she'd believed with almost religious zeal that the fire could satisfy her deepest curiosities, that in its furtive flickers she would glimpse nothing less than the meaning of the cosmos.

"Come forward," the priestess said again, and Vivian placed one stumbling foot after the next, the object of her endless quest burning before her like an indigo star.

There were those who said fire was an expression of the divine. There was Moses and the burning bush, the great "I AM"; there was Agni, the Hindu fire God, riding on the back of his goat with flaming hair flying in the wind; there was Vulcan, the Roman god of the forge, wielding his mighty blacksmith's hammer as he toiled in a supernatural inferno. Now, standing in the midst of this underground temple, Vivian believed all those stories were true.

The flames sang to her as they danced, casting harsh, abstract shadows along the walls, primal rhythmic chants promising salvation. Come, the fire crooned. Find the answers you seek.

A blinding flash erupted as Vivian stepped into the flames. They tore into her skin, which sizzled and crackled; they clawed at her eyes, which boiled and popped. Smoke choked her airways so she could no longer breathe. But none of that mattered, because here, on the precipice of death, the secrets of the universe were revealed to her at last.

"I see," Vivian rasped through blackened lips.

The fire required sacrifice, the priestess had said, and how right she'd been. The fire had opened her eyes, giving her the knowledge she desired, but, in return, it had demanded her life. That was how the World Fire worked, how it claimed the fuel it needed to burn, the fuel it needed to power every revolution of the Earth around the sun.

Vivian's body crumpled in immolation, and she offered her spirit to the fire and said no more.

Thread

IT WAS WITH HER for as long as she could remember, a thin, golden thread of light that tugged at her as if she were a hooked fish. She had no idea where it came from or where it led. She only knew that it was always pulling—that with every passing year, the tightness increased until the pain was too much to bear.

Nobody else could see it. Not her mother or father, not her relatives, not her friends. It got to be so bad that she spent most days alone, afraid others would think she was crazy.

On her eighteenth birthday, the pain blossomed into searing fire. Not knowing what else to do, she left home, left everyone and everything she'd ever known behind. She followed the pull of the thread out of Phoenix, out of Arizona, out of the US. Traveling helped; the thread slackened when she followed. She spent most of her life allowing it to drag her across the world, never knowing where or if it would end.

Now, after more than forty years of never staying in one place, she stands before a small redbrick house in Belgium and knows that she's come home. She sees that the golden thread leads here, that inside the house there is an even brighter glow. This is where her journey ends.

She swallows, takes a deep breath, walks up, and knocks on the door. There's a brief moment where she wonders what she'll do if it doesn't open, and then it does. Gold floods her vision.

"Come in," says a kindly voice. "I've been waiting for you."

She enters. The door closes behind her.

High Fantasy

Introduction

Believe it or not, my desire since about the end of high school (circa 2002, when dinosaurs roamed the Earth) was to write epic fantasies that took place in a pseudo-medieval setting. I spent years building my world. After taking a bunch of math and science classes in college, I even devised a magic system that extended real-world physics and was defined mathematically (I might repurpose this for something else, because it would be a terrible shame to waste it...). However, life, as it so often does, forced me to take detours down unexpected avenues, and before I knew what was happening, I'd fallen in love with writers like Stephen King[1] and Neil Gaiman, and thus my love affair with modern fantasy began.

I wrote "The Last Heir" somewhere between 2006 and 2008, back when my interest in high fantasy was at its peak. Later, I revised and repurposed it for my blog. There's something special about reaching so far back in time, finding a story you'd thought would be forever relegated to your private shelf, pulling it out into the light, and sharing it with the world at last. As a then frustrated writer who believed nothing of his would ever be published, it now feels like I've come full circle.

"Best Friends," "Through the Flame," and "Training" were written more recently. To this day, high fantasy holds a special place in my heart, and, while it's no longer my focus, I like to flirt with the genre every now and then and, with a glass of wine in hand[2], remember the old times.

---

[1] Actually, I originally discovered Stephen King during my first two years in high school, then fell out of love with his work for a while. Coming back to his books was a renaissance for me, and I've been a hopeless fan-boy ever since.

[2] Full disclosure: I like the expression, but don't actually like the taste of wine.

Best Friends

Don stood outside a pair of broad double doors. Torches in iron sconces along the walls cast a dim orange glow in the late-night darkness. At his word, the doors would open, and then he would carry out his duty. But for now, he waited.

The night was cool, serene. The chirrups of crickets, the rustling of treetops, spoke a comforting lie. They told the story of a world whole and intact, of a world untouched by the atrocities of a civil war that had almost destroyed humanity itself. Don wanted to steep in its sweet murmurs, to find what refuge he could in the all-too-brief illusion.

But Don had a job to do, one that shouldn't wait any longer than necessary. After a dusty, bone-weary sigh, he signaled to the guards.

The doors opened.

Light flooded out from a humongous palatial chamber, a coruscating electric blue. No illusions here. Tapestries lay in tatters on the floor alongside clotted blood and broken bodies, strewn about as if toys abandoned by a spoiled child.

At the center, where the light originated, was a man in a sword-torn uniform, about the same age as Don. He had snow-capped hair and a permanent frown line, etched by time and turmoil into a face that could no longer move, save for the lips. Presently, those lips were curled into a sour grimace of disgust.

Don could see that, even now, the man fought against his restraints. It was a futile effort, of course, and the man knew it as well as he.

Don approached, the light beginning to thicken like gel around him. Not too close, his advisers had warned. The light was a trap. It was how they'd captured the man who stood before Don now. If he got too close, it would harden around him just like it had his prisoner.

"It's been a while," said Don, after searching for words appropriate to the occasion and coming up short. A headache was blooming in his left temple, and his stomach had started to churn. The sight of his best friend, Arnold, bound by the light, no matter how evil he'd turned out to be, still rattled the cage around his weary soul with grief.

Arnold sneered but did not answer.

"You destroyed my kingdom. You destroyed the world. It will take centuries to rebuild."

The sneer widened.

Don shivered, and the light around them turned a darker shade of blue. *Who was this man?* They'd grown up together in the castle, and though Don had been a prince destined for the throne, and Arnold had been a servant destined for the stables, he'd loved the boy like a brother and had treated him likewise. But this man couldn't be the same person he'd grown up with. Couldn't be the same. *Couldn't* be the same.

Yet here he was.

"Why?" It was not the question Don had meant to ask, but it bubbled out of him anyway, with all the force of an active volcano. "Why, Arnold? I trusted you. I *loved* you." His voice cracked around the word love. "You were part of the family."

When Arnold didn't answer, Don raised his voice. "Do you not know I have the power to destroy you? Answer me!"

No reply. The light flared.

Don's hands trembled at his sides. Love, he reflected, was a dangerous thing. Wonderful, exhilarating, at times liberating, but dangerous all the same. He had loved his friend Arnold, had welcomed him into the royal house as an equal, and a broken world had been the result.

The light's shade darkened once more, and Don felt a love already starved by the horrors of war dwindle further like a guttering ember. It cried out in its death throes, interceding on his friend's behalf, but ultimately fell on deaf ears.

"By order of the Crown and in defense of the Common Realm, I sentence you to death."

Don snapped his fingers, and the light rushed inward, coalescing around Arnold, crystallizing around him, flesh and bone. Arnold's mouth twisted into a final derisive grin, then opened wide as he let out a muffled, agonized death cry. He arched his back, pulled taut by the matrix of light turned substance, then cried no more.

Why did you do this, old friend?

Don would live the rest of his life without the answer.

The light died, leaving behind a block of stone with Arnold's body encased inside, and Don's childhood heart died along with it.

The Last Heir

TIEN WALKED ALONG a grassy plain, bathed in moonlight. In the distance stood a ruined castle, the final defiant cry of a long-gone age. Once a fortified structure crafted by the greatest of rulers, it was now nothing more than a weathered collection of broken walls and battered gates.

Tien approached the drawbridge, face covered with mud and sweat, clothes torn, streaked and stained. He gazed up at the massive structure, turned dreamily from one crumbled and broken gate tower to the next.

A low rumble sounded from within and the massive bridge tumbled to the ground. Tien made his way across, rickety panels of ancient wood creaking beneath his feet.

He passed through the gate and emerged on the other side of a forgotten world, a wide-open space that had once been occupied by laboring serfs and peasants. Now it stood empty and alone.

He continued past the inner ward, all the while clutching the handle of his sword, constructed according to the tenets of an ancient craft that had died along with the castle. He passed the remains of what had once been the great hall, then finally stood before the keep.

Here all four turrets still stood, untouched by the ages. It seemed that not even time had breached the castle walls entirely. Tien slipped through the open doors. He marched in the dark across a faded red carpet, past moth-eaten banners and flags, and stopped when he reached the throne. There he knelt and closed his eyes.

A wind gusted, blowing through the room, and for a moment the banners of a forgotten kingdom flapped once more. Then the keep flooded with golden light, and when Tien looked up he saw the King, holding audience from the throne.

Tien's gaze fell to the floor. The King, gazing down at him in solemn understanding, removed his crown and placed it atop Tien's head. A flaccid smile grazed the old man's lips.

Tien rose to his feet, spared a final regretful gaze for the world beyond. Then the room darkened, and once more the ruins stood in silence.

The castle had claimed its heir.

Through the Flame

ANITA THREW MORE WOOD onto what was already a blazing fire. Glowing embers popped and cracked, leaping into the air like fireworks. That should be enough, she thought. She sat on the smooth white sand to watch the flames. So far, the beach was barren, save for herself. But that wouldn't be the case for very long.

A few hundred yards ahead, where land met water, the ocean smacked into a pile of rocks, sending up a jet of misty white spray.

She was sure she'd been followed. She'd taken precautions, but the soldiers who pursued her were seasoned trackers, and she was certain they were at most a few hours behind.

Before her, bright orange flames reached for the sky like earthbound spirits, flickering in the confines of a crude stone ring. She stared at the place where the air shimmered from the heat, a flame-induced mirage, and concentrated. She could feel it, drawn to her through the fire like iron toward a magnet: the mirror world, which like her own would die without her help.

The mirage flickered. Dimmed. She pushed through the partition with her mind, picked at the boundary between worlds. She gave a relieved sigh when the dimness subsided, resolving into a beach very much like her own.

There, in the mirror world, was an identical fire, and beside it an alternate Anita was seated before the flames with her eyes closed.

Suddenly breathless and eager to be done, she reached into a small leather satchel and retrieved a faded parchment, rolled and sealed with her family crest. She reached toward her alter ego, who had opened her eyes and was now simultaneously reaching out with her own hand. She pushed through the partition, feeling like her hand had been submerged in gel. They exchanged notes, pulled away, and, just like that, the bridge between their worlds evaporated.

Just as Anita came back to herself she heard horses' hooves, pounding against the sand like distant thunder. It seemed her enemies were closer than she'd thought. No matter. The deed was done. She'd saved mirror-Anita's world, and in so doing had saved her own.

She opened the scroll, read her alter ego's note and smiled.

Let them come.

She would be ready.

Training

John hears a sound. Turns.

Click, click.

It's coming. He wheels around and takes off through the tunnel. He can still hear it as it closes in. He doesn't dare look back again. Looking back means slowing down, and slowing down means dying.

Click, click.

He hardly registers the foul miasma that hangs over the dungeon, a putrid sulfuric rot, though it took him aback when he first entered the place.

When was that?

He tries to remember, but whenever he reaches back in time, it's like slamming into a metal curtain. All he knows is that he's being pursued and he has to get away.

There are brief flashes in the dim surroundings like a strobe, flickers of a life before the dungeon. Colors and lights. Flowers and trees. A family. Kids. But none of these ever resolve into the fully clothed specters of memory.

CLICK, CLICK.

It's almost on top of him now. Perhaps thirty yards away, maybe twenty. John's heart hammers in his chest. He can feel a strangely familiar power blossoming inside, a latent ability to do…something, an ability that only expresses itself when he's in danger. That power is important. He knows it as a matter of instinct. There's something he has to remember, something crucial. He has to—

Claws clamp down into his back, and an impossible weight sends him tumbling to the ground. The foul water that was at his feet splashes into his nostrils, so that he feels for a moment like he's drowning.

Meanwhile, he can feel the creature on top of him, pushing, tearing, lacerating his upper back, shredding it to blood-soaked ribbons. John screams and the sound bounces off the walls in an endless cascade of agony.

Every nerve has come alive, like cables that send thousands of volts coursing through his body. He can feel the power within, pulsing, waiting for him to take hold. Yet he doesn't know how, and with each feeble attempt it fumbles away from his grasp and bounds off into the dark. And then the creature's humid maw has opened wide above him, breathing its stink over the back of his neck. John screams again.

More pain. Then darkness.

JOHN SURGES BACK INTO CONSCIOUSNESS, crying out as the final drops of world-shattering torment drain out of him.

When it's over, he stops. Rises. Looks around.

He now finds himself in a small stone chamber, surrounded by brightly burning candles. Beside him, eyes closed, kneels an old woman, her face obscured by harsh lines and shadows.

"Where am I?"

The woman answers without opening her eyes. "Give it a moment to come back."

And as if her words were a command, the curtain in his head parts.

"Oh, no," he says, and he drops his head into his hands. "I failed again."

"Stuff and nonsense," says the old woman. "You still have a ways to go, it's true, but you're not a failure."

"I still couldn't do it. The power, I felt it inside of me, but I couldn't figure out how to handle it."

"Perhaps not," she agrees, "but you sensed it, and that's a start. We've been through this exercise a thousand times before. Until today, you'd never even realized it was there. Something changed this iteration. You sensed it, and you knew you had to reach for it. You've improved very much."

"What use is it if I can only sense it?"

"You have to sense it before you can use it."

John looks up, stares at the old woman beside him. She's now opened her eyes. "I'm scared."

"We all are," she says. "These are dark times. But you're learning. Sooner or later, you'll master it. Sooner or later, you'll reach for it without thinking, and that's very important, because when the peril is real, when the Chancellor steals your memory in earnest and throws you into his pit to play his game, the power will be your only advantage."

"I want to go again. Please," he says, "Let me go again."

"You need rest."

"Just one more time."

She stares into his eyes, and she must see something burning in their gaze, for when she speaks again, she gives her reluctant assent.

"Just once more. Then off to bed."

John nods, relieved. His contest is a month away. If he can survive, if he can beat the Chancellor's game, perhaps the man will grant him an audience. It would be the first time the Chancellor has allowed it in fifteen hundred years. And then, well, anything is possible.

"Close your eyes," says the old woman, not unkindly, and he does as he's told.

Once more, a fog settles over his mind, and the neurons in his head realign. The curtain closes. And then he's in the dungeon, running, trying to get away.

Click, click.

Writing

Introduction

"The Magic Returns" was written shortly after my wedding, when I was busy and wasn't able to write for a while. As a writer, you grow rusty and unsure of yourself quickly, and that story was my attempt to reconnect with my art. "Regret," meanwhile, was in some sense a reflection of how I used to be before I started to take my writing seriously, back when my depression was at an all-time high and I didn't have the courage or the conviction to get anything done.

The stories in this category all talk in some way about writing and its power as an artistic medium, and all are, to various degrees, surreal and symbolic (a few so much so that they're effectively fantasy).

Creator of Worlds

I SEE IT glimmering beneath the surface of the universe in an unformed realm that precedes creation. It is primordial, a complex composition of ageless utterances transcending language, space, and time. I hunch over a stack of paper with my pen in hand, ready to surround it with a net of words. They are crude in their expressive power, yet capable enough to capture its essence, trap its soul so I can slowly reel it in, a whole new world, young and still crackling with newborn magic.

I am thought of by most as a creator of worlds. But I am only a lowly fisherman, trawling an insubstantial ocean in search of worlds half-glimpsed, eternal mysteries even to the likes of me. I make my modest living on the few small worlds I'm strong enough to catch. I glimpse larger ones, great hulking cosmos buried deep beneath the depths. But even as I reach for them, I know that I'm too weak, that my net is too shallow to ever catch them.

That is perhaps the most frustrating part of what I do, to spy so many nascent worlds flitting through the ether that will forever remain unexpressed, doomed to an everlasting half-life in the shadow of nonexistence. I weep for them, but there is nothing I can do.

I turn away from such thoughts to gaze at my latest acquisition. It is beautiful, resplendent. I love it like a newborn child.

Then I catch another glimmer.

Regret

THERE IS NO GREATER PUZZLE, no greater struggle, than the beginning. The first note of a sonata, the first stanza of a poem, the first stroke of a painting. All that comes after builds on what came before, and if the scaffolding established at the start is weak, the whole piece comes tumbling down.

It was the reason I never put my own skills to use, the reason my house had always been a tangled jungle of loose-leaf pages, saturated with ideas I never had the courage to pursue.

I would come home from work, bleary-eyed and broken. I would descend the shadow-engulfed stairs that led to my desk beneath the moldering ceiling of a neglected basement, and there, in the dark, I would set pen to paper. For a little while, I would labor under the delusion that this time, things would be different; this time, I would follow through with my design; this time, I would impart substance and life to an idea that I was certain could change the world.

Then I would stare at the latest fruit of my manic-depressive mind, pondering its intricacies, its peculiarities. I would sigh, turn out the light, and go to bed, abandoning my brainchild to rot along with the house's foundation.

Time slipped and I grew old. I never stopped telling myself that this time, things would be different. But one day, I fell ill, and after an extended stay in the hospital I realized I wasn't going home. On the precipice of death, I thought of all my unfinished designs, and like an absent father, I wailed and lamented for all the lost years that I could never reclaim with my children.

Better to have tried, I thought. Better to have started something imperfectly than not to have started at all. But somehow that was worse, somehow that was more painful.

"I loved you all," I whispered, but as I closed my eyes, as the final curtain began to fall on my life, I realized with mounting terror that this was a lie.

The Generous Patron

"**D**AMN."

Alan sighed and dropped his hands. A moment later, the half-formed construction of fire that hovered before him vanished. Without its flickering light, the market stall was cold and dark.

He'd tried to make a Phoenix. Not an actual living creature that could take to the sky, but a forging of elemental magic, a work of art, a tribute to nature's greatest and most breathtaking creature.

But nobody had come to visit. Nobody had come to see his spectacular figures of ice and fire, so what did it matter that he hadn't gotten this last one right?

His big brother's words came back to him.

There's no money in magic. Go out and find a real job.

But Alan had been young and idealistic. He believed the world needed magic, that without its beauty and the awe that it inspired, life wasn't worth living. Now Alan thought that maybe his brother had been right all along. Maybe there was no place for his kind of talent.

Cold and alone, Alan started packing up for the night.

He was about to unravel the cord that anchored his tent to the ground when a soft female voice startled him.

"I'd like to see what you have to offer."

Alan spun, almost knocked into a nearby table, and spied a young woman dressed in a dark coat; here eyes caught the light of distant lanterns and seemed to glow.

"Sorry, ma'am," he said, catching his breath. "I'm closing."

"That's a shame."

"You wouldn't be interested anyway," said Alan, years of bitterness rising to the fore. "Just worthless avatars, nothing of actual value."

"I'd like to be the judge of what I find interesting."

A breeze swept through the dwindling market, kicking up dried leaves, yet the fabric of her coat remained untouched. There was something about her stately presence that unnerved him, and he felt suddenly as if he were dreaming.

"I only dabble in magic," he found himself saying, averting his gaze. "Surely you'd prefer something of more practical value."

"I happen to like magic."

He stared at her for a moment, then nodded. *Fine.* He could cycle through a few forms.

When she tired of his art, he could send her on her way and be that much closer to going home.

"All right," he said, and he sat down before the broad oak table he'd almost toppled a moment before.

What should he make for her? He tried to think of something captivating, but found he was too self-conscious to think clearly.

As if sensing his vulnerability, she sat down on an empty chair across from him and took one of his hands into her own.

"Go on," she insisted. "Form whatever's in your heart."

Now the light in her eyes radiated patience and kindness, and he found a comfort so unexpectedly powerful that the walls inside his head began to weaken.

Whatever was in his heart… He supposed he could do that. He didn't know this woman, but in this intimate moment that passed between them, he was certain he could trust her, that he would be safe expressing a piece of his truest self.

Alan closed his eyes.

The form that leaped to mind nearly arrested him with heart-stopping wonder. An expression of vulnerability and longing, of an age-old passion, once dusty and dry, its dying flames stoked at last.

His hands started to move, animated by a force not entirely his own. The woman, the tent, the other stalls, they all fell away, burned to ash before a blinding interior vision. The form he beheld was a soul without a body, an essence in need of life. Alan was the vessel through which it could achieve that life, and he was eager to fulfill its need. He reached beyond himself, beyond the world, into the vast, limitless universe and its roiling sea of unrealized power and potential.

He channeled that boundless reservoir of energy, dividing what he took into its constituent parts. From one, he drew scintillating fibers of bright, orange fire—serpentine tongues that lashed through the air in bright, sparkling flashes. From another, he drew frosty tendrils of ice, subliming into the wind in gentle, billowing wisps like smoke.

Then, like an artisan weaver, he wound these two elemental threads together into a single seamless fabric, a bold, exotic material of contrast and extremes. When he'd spun enough, he tied it off, held it suspended in the air, a lump of clay to be molded and shaped, and refined with each pass of his deft and dexterous hands.

The basic form complete, he reached out once more and spun invisible threads of wind and air. These became the life force that would bind the whole together.

Finished at last.

Alan opened his eyes. The world came back into focus, and he almost jumped when he saw the woman sitting close to him. He'd been so lost in what he was doing he'd forgotten she was there.

Above both their heads, there now hovered a bright, fiery dragon, shot through with strands of icy blue; its broad wings flapped in the air, sending down heavy gusts of frigid winter wind as well as hot, baking heat. A masterpiece.

The woman clapped her hands.

"It's wonderful!" she exclaimed. "The best I've ever seen."

Alan blushed. "Thank you. It's not much, but it's the best I can do."

Alan let the elemental form persist until he felt the fibers begin to buckle, eager to be released. Sadly, regretfully, he let the cord that anchored him to his creation go. The dragon above their heads vanished in a puff of smoke.

"It is everything," she said, with such gravity that he was taken aback. "There are those who do practical things, and they are important, because without them the world cannot function. There are also those who do beautiful things, and they, too, are important, because without them the world cannot remember why it functions."

Tears sprung to Alan's eyes as the idealist of his youth burst from its hard, cynical shell.

"You are a maker of beautiful things," she continued. "You are important and necessary, and I would like to be your patron, if you would have me."

"My— What?" Alan's heart seemed to stop.

She wanted to be his patron. He nearly trembled with shock.

"Your magic must live on. You won't survive here, in this world of practical things. You were made for a different life, and I would like to be the one who makes that life possible."

"Thank you," he whispered, his voice suddenly husky and hoarse. "Thank you."

"Come on," she said. "I'll help you tear down. We have a lot to discuss."

I wrote this as a way to thank my patrons after a very successful Patreon campaign. If you're a patron who's reading this, let me say it again: THANK YOU!

The Magic Returns

HE SITS IN A COLD, dark corner, alone and afraid. It's been too long, he thinks. He's like an ancient, dried-out riverbed, where the magic hasn't flowed for ages. What makes him think he can summon it now?

Once, he was capable of great things. Through his unique talent, entire worlds emerged from nothing, whatever his heart and mind could conceive. He took it for granted, thinking it would always be there to serve him.

But he was soon swept up by worldly concerns. He stopped using the magic, stopped creating, and though the fire inside never stopped burning, it grew small and ashen through a chronic lack of practice. He was too busy with work, he told himself, too busy trying to feed his family, too busy doing a hundred other things. Only later, when it seemed too late, did he realize those were excuses, that he could have retreated to his study for as little as five minutes at a time, because there were always pockets of time to be found if only one was dedicated enough to search for them.

He hasn't created for so long now that the channels through which the magic once flowed have closed up. It's too late, he thinks. Only the fire inside still burns, no longer just a pile of dying embers as they'd been for so many years, but a raging inferno.

He sits at his old desk because he doesn't know what else to do.

"Is this what you want?" he whispers to nobody in particular, "To mock me? To remind me that I gave up?" Mad with grief, he hardly knows what he's saying.

Anguish reaches a climax. He feels small and helpless, like an ant caught up in a sandstorm. There's nothing to lose anymore, only an ache that will grow deeper and fuller the longer he stays away.

He reaches into the void and at long last does the only thing he's ever known how to do.

He closes his eyes and opens himself to the magic.

At first, nothing comes. In a moment of despair, he's certain his worst fears have been confirmed. But then he hears it building as if from a great distance, and the shriveled conduits in his mind quiver with anticipation. The dam breaks, and the dried-up riverbed floods once more, a raging current of pent up magic he thought forever inaccessible.

He doesn't know how long he's been sitting in the dark before the colossal torrent finally ebbs. When he comes back to himself, he stares at his latest creation, mute and disbelieving.

At last, a work of art he can call his own.

Tears blur his vision as he realizes the truth—that the magic never left him. He turned his back on it for a while, but it was always there, waiting for him to embrace it. Like a guiding star, it reorients him. Old priorities wither before a renewed sense of purpose.

For the first time in decades, he can call himself an artist.

The Writer

J ARED'S EYES POPPED open at 3:17 in the morning. His head was pounding. His brain was a jumbled kaleidoscope of broken thoughts and disjointed memories, and at first he couldn't tell where he was.

Then the pressure in his head increased. Jared moaned. He tossed the blanket aside, fumbled in the dark for the light switch, then walked briskly to his desk and picked up a pen. He groped the hardwood surface for his notebook. When he found it, he pulled it open to where he'd left off that afternoon.

Jared began to write.

Images of a life not his own funneled slowly from his mind, through his hand, and onto the paper beneath him. It was dizzying, looking through two pairs of eyes at the same time. He was Jared, the writer who lived alone in a one-bedroom apartment. He was Arthur, a balding art mogul in his mid-forties, gulping for air as his studio partner plunged a six-inch serrated knife into his back.

As he scribbled furiously, trying to relieve the pressure, he wondered if he was writing the story or if the story was writing him.

He'd never asked for this. One day in high school, he'd been sitting in his sixth-period English class when a story had come plummeting out of nowhere. It seized control of his senses, then raped him repeatedly as he sat there helpless in front of his teacher and his peers. All he could do was write it down, scribbling in his three-ring binder so fast that he nearly tore several pages, hoping and praying that somehow he could get it out of his head without anybody noticing that he was no longer paying attention.

Since then, his life had been a never-ending series of unpredictable encounters.

After a time, the wellspring ran dry. His viewfinder into Arthur's soul vanished, and he was left gasping for air with his head in his hands. After taking a few minutes to catch his breath, he turned out the light. He returned to the covers, drenched in sweat, and he prayed. He asked God (if there was a God) to take this from him, though all the while he knew his prayer was in vain.

I wrote this story after an as-of-yet unfinished novel, originally titled The Writer, *but later re-named* Purely Coincidental.

Patreon Exclusives

Introduction

For the moment, my primary means of financial support for the books I write comes through Patreon, a platform where I post four additional pieces of flash fiction per month in exchange for a small recurring pledge. Until this book, Patreon was the only place where you could find these stories, but I've decided to include a few of my favorites here.

Blue

The stone had always been blue. Since time unremembered it had sat, polished and round, mounted in the center of the city. The people would go out in the middle of the night when it shone most brightly, and in the presence of that otherworldly glow, they would kneel and pay it homage.

It was their bedrock, the binding force that kept them civilized. A covenant between man and the infinite. So when the stone stopped giving its light, when the city's streets went dark for the first time in recorded history, chaos loomed.

"It's the end of the world!" they wailed. "The Gods have abandoned us."

The priests tried to maintain order.

"Calm yourselves," they said, taking up defensive positions around the stone. "It is only a test. We must be steadfast in our faith. Then the Gods will show us their favor once more."

The people grumbled, restless and uneasy, but, one by one, they returned to their homes, some to pray, others to brood in silent worry.

The following night, they approached the center of the city. Once more, they saw the stone was dark.

They turned to the priests and asked, "What explanation will you offer us now?" They were wild-eyed, terrified, and half out of their minds.

Once more, the priests tried to maintain order.

"Calm yourselves," they said. "The test has not ended. Be strong and keep the faith of our ancestors."

"The Gods have abandoned us!" they cried. "What use are you now?"

"Be still," the priests admonished. "The Gods have done no such thing. Return tomorrow, and you will see for yourselves that the stone gives light once more."

Again the people grumbled. Some challenged them further, some even threatened violence if the stone was not restored to its former state as had been promised.

The priests watched them turn back, watched them disappear like apparitions, and, inwardly, they trembled. They had not a clue why the stone went dark, nor when it would share its light again.

"Please," they implored together through a formal rite of prayer that hadn't been invoked for more than a thousand years. "We beseech thee, the Gods of our ancestors, return to us thy divine light so that order might be restored."

Exhausted and afraid, they retired to their quarters to sleep.

That night, the children of the city dreamed. They saw the pillars of their civilization crumble, saw their elders perish in an all-consuming fire that seemed to rise from the bowels of the Earth. An ancient cycle was nearing its end, and in that dream, a voice urged them to run if they would be a part of the next.

They each woke in a cold sweat, eyes lit with terror. But none spoke of the strange vision until much later.

The third night approached. The priests went out ahead of the crowd and observed with growing terror that the stone was still dark. They held the people back with exhortations of prayer, but, in the end, they could delay them no longer.

When the people beheld that infernal darkness, the priests tried once more to pacify them. But the citizens of the city were enraged. They were certain now the Gods had abandoned them, and all their priests could do was offer empty promises of salvation.

"The Gods have defied your predictions," one man cried, "yet you would stand here and assure us all is well. We're through with your lies!"

The people attacked.

The children, left behind by parents who'd already feared the streets would grow violent, heard a whisper ride in on the coattails of the wind.

Get out. Find safety outside the city walls and don't return until the next full moon.

One by one, they filtered out into the dark.

Meanwhile, the people, having sacrificed their priests, turned on each other. A frantic, desperate bloodlust had filled their eyes and they were overtaken by an urgent need to destroy. They swept through the city like a plague, looting, murdering, burning buildings to the ground, so that in the end only a single person remained. In his final moments, he gazed up at the moon, mad with lunatic understanding, and ran himself through with his sword.

ON THE NEXT FULL MOON, the children crept back to the ruins of their city as the voice had told them. They passed the skeletal remains of their homes, the stinking, bloated bodies of their dead parents. The younger ones threw up. The older ones took them into their arms and led them away.

They found the stone, standing in the center as it always had. They gathered around it and lifted their voices in prayer. For a moment, there was only the wind, which whistled through broken archways and windows like a ghost. Then there was a flicker and a flash. They opened their eyes. The stone was blue once more. The children offered thanks.

In the morning, the older ones started to rebuild.

The land's thirst for blood had been sated.

The new cycle had begun.

Forerunner

Though the road is long and you cannot find your way, keep your head up. Don't you see? I've been where you are. I know all too well the pain. The fear. The despair. I experienced the dark night of the soul, and I survived.

If you could only see what awaits you on the other side of time… You are on the cusp of a fundamental transformation, a changing of body and matter into light and energy. All the treasures of the stars can be yours, if only you have the strength to go on.

I was the first of many, the forerunner, and I have returned to tell you this: What I am, so will you become.

Just Doing His Job

HE SLIPPED INSIDE THE CHURCH, unseen; sat down in a nearby pew and waited. It was an old stone cathedral, erected in the Philippines by Spanish Catholics during the 1600s. He paused to admire the architecture and took a mental snapshot. He'd never been to the Philippines before, and he was pretty sure he wouldn't be going back.

Every now and then he turned to peer at one of the three broad double doors. He was waiting for someone.

Ten or fifteen minutes of contemplative silence. Then he spotted an elderly woman in a faded blue blouse. He watched closely as she knelt to pray, and, after a brief appraisal, his suspicions were confirmed.

It was subtle, something that most people either couldn't see or didn't bother to notice. A slight ripple, a liquid shimmer in the air, like a mirage in the distance on a hot summer day. In her presence, things would change in almost imperceptible ways, a brief tweaking of probabilities and outcomes. Some things would become a little more likely, others a little bit less.

Such individuals had effected profound changes in the course of human events, small alterations to reality that rippled outward into space and time, having an increasingly heavy impact on the world and beyond. Most had no idea what they were capable of, and, of those who did, rarer still were those who could control it. It was simply a part of their nature, a manifestation of their existence.

Now that she was praying, her influence had grown strong. He could see it swirling all around her.

He got to his feet and quietly approached her from behind. It was best to avoid a confrontation, to avoid getting caught in her web of influence.

He reached into a coat pocket and produced a small pen-like object and pad of paper. Then he positioned the pen-like object so that it was pointed at the woman's neck. Finally he pushed down on a spring-loaded button. An instant later, the woman swatted at her neck.

When she turned to investigate the source of the sting, he smiled and pretended to scribble words into his notebook. Confused, she returned his smile with one of her own and turned back to face the tabernacle and continue praying.

The sting would have been benign. She would have forgotten about it even before she turned back toward the front of the church. She would go home after mass, have dinner with her family, fall asleep at the end of the day, and, by morning, her family would be planning her funeral.

He punctuated an empty page, placed the pen-like object back into his pocket along with the notebook, and exited the church. The humid heat of Bacolod embraced him.

He had just been doing his job, and this one was done. Tomorrow, he would board a morning flight for Manila; an hour later, he would be flying out to California.

He had another job to do.

Masterpiece

A IDEN LOOKED DOWN at the lump of clay in his hands. He had a vision for it, at least in the abstract, a progression from raw material to masterpiece that he thought he'd have no trouble achieving. But now, here he was, with nothing but a crudely executed parody to show for his hours of molding, scraping, picking, and pulling. The useless object before him lacked that spark of life his mentor had always infused into his own creations so effortlessly.

He took it into his hands, beheld it like a disapproving father, and threw it across the workshop, where it thudded against the wood paneled wall and clattered into a pile of empty canisters.

Why was it so hard? His mentor had lectured him over and over again about how difficult it was, about how frustrating and time-consuming and painful it could be. But being young and brash, he'd vowed to accomplish great things right out of his apprenticeship. Yet Aiden had spent more than six months on his first solo project, and he'd produced nothing more than a misshapen blob of clay.

"Don't strive for perfection," his mentor had said. "Your projects will never live up to the visions you have for them. But if you accept them as they are, if you choose to love them, not in spite of, but *because* of their flaws and imperfections, you'll find they live up to something better." That would be his most painful lesson, he'd concluded, one that Aiden would have to learn for himself when he set out to do his own work.

Aiden sighed, rested his head in his hands to collect his thoughts. He supposed he was learning that lesson now, and it was indeed hard. He knew exactly what it was he wanted to create. Buried deep inside his head was a near-immaculate conception of the life he wanted to create, and then his hands, fallible and unsure, had betrayed him. His hands were like infants struggling to walk, or school children struggling to read. The operations all seemed so basic and elementary, yet his hands were incapable of carrying them out, at least to the precision that he so desperately desired.

But then perhaps art wasn't about imposing your will on the canvas, but releasing the life within. Perhaps the clumsiness and the imperfections were the means by which the work gained an identity of its own, apart from its creator; perhaps it was already endowed with the very life Aiden had been struggling to achieve through brute force.

At any rate, what was he going to do, sit here beneath the dim illumination of his candles and sulk, or accept and perhaps even make peace with his limitations and get to work? If he chose the latter, then, even if he failed, at least he would know that he'd done his best, at least he would have something to show for his effort. There would be a sense of finality, a closure that would allow him to move on to the next project. He thought if nothing else, at least his mentor would have been proud of him for that.

He rose from his seat, walked across the room to where his partial creation lay abused and neglected on the floor. He bent down to retrieve it, apologetic, and carried the sculpture back to his workbench. As he gazed down at it beneath the candlelight, he was seized by an unexpected love, like a father with a son who fails but tries so hard to please. At first the work was awkward, something he had to force himself to do. But after the next fifteen or twenty minutes, a curious thing happened. The project before him was transformed, became not a burden and an obligation, but a joy, a hope for things to come.

He spent the next several days in a fevered effort, molding, then painting, letting his initial vision filter down through clumsy hands and fingers, improvising where necessary, letting it take on a form all its own. Now he could feel the life flowing through him, from his soul, through his fingertips, and into his work.

At last, in the middle of the night on a cold winter day, his creation was complete. He gazed upon a masterpiece born of love, dumbstruck as it spread its wings and ruffled its feathers, showing off great rainbow plumage, the likes of which had never been seen before, nor would ever be seen again.

True, it didn't live up to the vision in his head, but, as his mentor had promised, through its flaws and imprecision, it lived up to something better.

It craned its neck. Took to the air. Aiden unlatched and opened the window, and out it went, launching toward the stars, glowing like a shooting star. He had given it what he could, and through his faith and effort it had done the rest on its own.

Aiden sat back, sweat beading on his forehead, and smiled. His mentor would have been proud.

Peace

A DEMONSTRATION OF POWER, they said. It will deter them. An arms race, our best magic against theirs, an arsenal that can destroy the world and assured retaliation against anyone foolish enough to attack. Peace, they said—those who had not known war for centuries but only its distant shadow. Weapons, power. They will ensure order and stability.

Now, the sun beats down on a barren land of stone and glass, silent like a tomb. There is no one left to wonder at this unearthly landscape, no one left to ask how such a thing could have happened.

They counted on the world to make sense. They said rationality and pragmatism would win the day. But they forgot that in man's heart, there is only chaos, that the world is a savage garden in which unpredictability is the only predictable outcome.

It is a mistake no one will be able to make again.

Quality Control

J OE SAT NEAR the final stretch of a massive assembly line that hummed contentedly in an unassuming brick-and-mortar factory. On one end, an industrial-sized funnel took as input a dark glob of empty space. On the other, a rubber conveyor belt delivered a steady stream of glowing white-hot stars.

So many stars. The boss had begun a new project, and Joe had been asked to work overtime.

Can't wait to get home and watch TV, thought Joe irritably as he glanced up at the clock on the wall. Just fifteen minutes remained of his twelve-hour shift. He supposed, all things considered, that his job wasn't half bad. The hours could be rough, but the boss was always generous in return. If only he could fill a more important role.

Contributing to the creation of a universe was kind of cool, but his part seemed so insignificant. He wasn't a designer, a planner, or an engineer, only a lowly grunt in quality control, sitting at the end of a big machine, watching as it regurgitated one celestial object after another.

He glanced at the clock again. Thirteen and a half minutes. He sighed, reached into a backpack beneath his chair, and pulled out a turkey sandwich.

Just as he was about to take a bite, there was a loud pop, like an engine backfiring. Acrid smoke began to plume from the assembly line. The steady hum gave way to the high-pitched whine of grinding gears and squealing belts. Startled, Joe dropped his sandwich and watched with horror as the machine began to output lifeless balls of lukewarm carbon.

He ran to maintenance for help, but found they'd clocked out for the day. Then he searched for an engineer, only to discover that they, too, had gone home. Panicking, he realized he was the only one left in the factory.

There was only one more thing to try. Taking a deep breath, he returned to maintenance, found the blueprints for the machine and located the proper tools. He'd spent some time observing the maintenance guys, watching over their shoulders as they serviced the mysterious black box that had suddenly failed without warning. Ironically, he'd hoped at the time to move into a department that saw a little more action. He had some idea of what the task entailed, but to actually do it himself...

Again he panicked. What if he made things worse? But he had to try. Those who were qualified wouldn't clock in again until tomorrow, and, by then, the boss's supply of empty space would be depleted. A delay at this stage could set them back eons.

Poring over the schematics, Joe determined the deactivation sequence and stopped the assembly line. Then he poked his head inside the black box and inspected the system. It was slow work, having to constantly refer to the documentation, but eventually he found it: a regulating belt that had snapped, causing the system to misfire. He went back to maintenance, found a spare belt, and spent the next three hours taking the machine apart.

Once he'd removed and replaced the belt, he spent another five hours putting the whole thing back together, all the while, sweating buckets, terrified he'd break something. He paused for a moment when he was finished to gaze at his handiwork, sleep-deprived and afraid. What if he turned it on and the damn thing exploded? But it was too late for second guesses.

He referred to the schematics one last time for the starting sequence, flipped a series of levers and switches, and held his breath as unseen parts began to clank and clatter to life once more. Gradually, the erratic sounds subsided, and the machine started to emit the soft, steady hum Joe had until today taken for granted. A moment later, bright burning stars began to emerge from the other side.

Joe exhaled loudly, fell back into his seat, and wiped his forehead with the back of a hand. Tomorrow, he would go to the boss and tell him what had happened.

Hopefully, he'd get a raise.

Shadows on the Wall

S AM PAUSED OUTSIDE the entrance to the monastery. He gazed up at the construction of coarse gray stones that reflected the pale unearthly glow of the moon above, peeked inside the tall glass windows that emitted the dull yellow of indoor candlelight. Was it really possible to speak with Melissa again? The mysteries of life and death circled each other inside his head, until he could bear it no longer.

He walked inside.

Though vandals had been present in the area for years, nobody bothered the monastery. Few were willing to pay it a visit, and even the monks avoided the chapel area during the night. Yet the door was always open, for there were still those poor souls who needed what only the chapel could provide.

Sam's footsteps echoed off the tiled floor. He peered at statues of the Apostles and the Virgin Mary, anxious and afraid. Would she hear his call and come? He needed to see her again. Needed to say goodbye.

He sat in one of the dusty wooden pews. A sound like a gunshot rang through the air and he jumped. But it was only the old wood popping beneath his weight. He let out a shaky breath, knelt, closed his eyes, and prayed.

"Melissa," he whispered. "I don't know if you can hear me. I'm afraid, but, Melissa, I miss you so much. I haven't been the same since you died. I need to see you again."

So many things he wanted to say. They got tangled up inside his head so that he couldn't find the words. In the end, he opened his eyes and sat back once more. He'd said all he needed to. If God willed it, if she wanted to come, that would be enough.

He watched his shadow on a nearby wall, large and looming, cast beyond the light of the flickering candles. He closed his eyes again. Took a deep breath. Opened his eyes.

His shadow was now joined by another. Startled, Sam turned, half expecting to see the rotten corpse of his dead wife reaching for him. But as far as he could tell, he was alone, all except for that second shadow on the wall.

The shadow of a woman.

His breath caught, and his heart leaped into his throat. "Melissa?" The word came out a feeble, winded croak.

The dark shape beside his own nodded.

Tears sprang to Sam's eyes. "Melissa," he whispered, "I've missed you. I—" He paused. There were so many things between them that had been left unspoken. But after a moment, he only reiterated what he'd said during his prayer. "I needed to say goodbye."

The shadow on the wall hung its head.

Sam rose to his feet and began to walk down the length of the aisle. Meanwhile, his shadow followed, along with the shadow of Melissa. When he stopped, he turned to see her wrap her arms around his shadow's two dimensional waist.

Sam longed to feel that touch, to feel the body that would have mirrored its movements in life. But that wasn't how the monastery worked. Some chasms were unbridgeable even here.

He opened his mouth to speak again, but what escaped was only a choked sob. Melissa. The pain was unbearable, and suddenly he wanted to turn and run, to flee into the night, far away from this cruel parody of life. But he couldn't do that to her. She'd come from the other side of death just to speak with him one last time. He had to be strong.

"Does death hurt?" he asked. "Should I be afraid?"

The dark profile on the wall smiled and shook its head.

"And are you happy?" he asked.

She nodded, still smiling.

More tears. Then another question occurred to him, scaring him more than any of the others.

"When I die, will we meet again?"

The shadow on the wall nodded. Yes, the gesture said. She would be there. He had nothing to fear.

"Thank you," Sam whispered. "I guess that's all I really needed. I love you."

The shadow on the wall grabbed his own, leaned in close, and kissed its insubstantial lips. And was that a breeze he felt, brushing against his mouth, or something more? He closed his eyes, savoring this final moment with the only woman he would ever love.

When he opened them, she was gone.

Sam fell into the nearest pew. Once more, the wood popped, but this time he wasn't startled. He knelt before the tabernacle, visions of their short time together flickering before his eyes.

When he left, the candles were only burned-out nubs, and the sun was poking up from the horizon.

"I love you," he said once more. "I can't wait to meet you again."

Surrender

"YOU FOUND ME."

"You weren't hard to find."

Arcturial nodded. He hadn't wanted to be caught exactly, but neither had he tried very hard to evade his captor.

"What happens next?" He looked toward the shadowy figure in the doorway.

The figure emerged into the soft, mystical glow of moonlight, resolving into a man of indeterminate features, skin tight and pallid, as if he donned a mask rather than a face.

"You come back with me," the man said, "and we return together to the Council."

Arcturial nodded again.

"Just as well. I'm tired. I don't want to run anymore."

"Five hundred years *is* a long time to be away from your kind."

"It is."

The man fell in beside him, and together they walked, boots clip-clopping through the darkened street. Arcturial flipped his gaze upward, finding the moon, white and luminescent. He drank in its otherworldly glow. He'd walked through hundreds of worlds, had existed long before the births of most, and still the vision was unlike anything else he'd seen before. He committed a snapshot to memory, for this would be the last time he saw it with his eyes.

"There will be punishment," said the man.

"I understand."

The echo of footfalls. Buildings rising before them, falling behind them.

"What was it like?"

Caught off-guard by the question, Arcturial stopped.

"What do you mean?"

"To live as a human. To feel, laugh, cry. What was it like?"

This was not a question he'd expected.

"Why do you ask?"

"Because," said the man, features set in a perpetually emotionless state, "there are those of us who envy what you've taken, even if we will never partake of it ourselves."

"I see."

Now, it was the other man's turn to nod.

How to sum up centuries of life in a human body that could never grow old or die? How to explain the desire and the need to feign mortality, to spend so many long years in the shadows, always on the outside looking in, knowing all you could ever do was pretend?

Arcturial thought before he spoke.

"Lonely."

"Ah," said the man.

Arcturial continued walking, and the man once more took up station beside him.

"I think we've gone far enough," said Arcturial. "We should be hidden from any mortals who might have seen us in the alley."

"Yes," the man agreed, "I think it's time to be on our way."

The two turned a corner, taking a detour that was neither north nor south, neither east nor west. The blackness of night enveloped them like a cloak, and the physical world melted away.

The 57

I SIT AT THE BUS STOP just before sunset and wait for the 57 to arrive. I'm the only one here, but that's not much of a surprise. Not many ride this bus anymore.

This city always used to be my home, but it's different now, and I hardly recognize it anymore. Nothing's changed on the surface. You can still see the old courthouse loom imposingly across the street from weathered concrete apartments that haven't seen a fresh coat of paint in thirty years. But the city's heart has undergone a strange transubstantiation that's left me alienated and as good as homeless.

They say the bus's purpose is to take care of people like me, people who've become vagrants in their own homes. Officially, the line stopped running sixteen years ago, but, every so often, someone goes to the abandoned stop, and at night, after the sounds of the vehicle have faded into the distance, they're never seen again. Now, I'm about to find out for myself exactly where it goes. Hell, the moon, outer space, doesn't matter. Anywhere is better than here.

The 57 pulls up at last, plastered with ads for products that no longer exist. It comes to a stop, issuing a hiss like steam. The doors swoosh open. I hesitate and take one last look around.

"You coming?" calls a gruff voice. The interior is consumed by shadows, so that I can only make out the driver's smoldering red eyes.

"Yes." My pulse quickens when I meet his gaze. I step inside, then jump as the doors swing shut. I take my seat. A moment later, the bus is rattling up to speed.

My former home recedes into the distance, and ahead there is only endless road.

The Wishing Pond

Eɪɢʜᴛ-ʏᴇᴀʀ-ᴏʟᴅ Jᴀɴᴇᴛ Gʀᴇᴇɴ stood beside the tranquil waters of the pond with silent, reverential wonder, like a nun before the tabernacle. Beside it towered an ancient, gnarled oak, its sprawling limbs reaching for the late-night sky. Above, the moon and the stars hung suspended in a black, cosmic sea.

The pond was her special place—the place where she went when she was trying to figure something out, the place she went when life got hard. Whenever someone said something mean at school, whenever she got yelled at for shirking her chores, whenever Mommy and Daddy fought, that was when she would slip out during the night and walk the narrow gravel road behind the family farm.

Today, Janet had hit another girl in class for calling her fat, and Mommy had picked her up from school.

"Go to your room," she said when they got home, lips tight. "I don't want to see you again until supper."

And Janet had done as she was told, tears spilling down red, puffy cheeks.

Now, she stared at the sky, pondering the mysteries that existed just beyond the shallow confines of Earth's atmospheric border. When she'd drunk her fill of empyrean secrets, she gazed down at the calm clear water, illuminated by the pale light of the moon, and tossed in a single quarter. A glowing ripple spread across the surface.

"I wish to soar among the stars."

When she was confident the pond had acknowledged her heart's desire, she bounded back to the house and went to sleep.

The reasons for Janet's visits changed as she grew older, but her wish remained the same. When she was in high school and had to decide if she should date Jimmy McCormick or Danny Stevens, when she was in college and she was afraid she wouldn't pass her final exams, when she got married, when she had her first and only child, when she lost her husband to war in the Middle East, each milestone brought her back to the special place of her youth.

"I wish to soar among the stars," she would say, and deep down she knew that someday her wish would come true, that the pond wouldn't forsake her.

Though Janet grew older and the world continued to spin, the pond beside the oak seemed perpetually unchanged, the only place in the world that was ever-present and eternal.

The evening she got her cancer diagnosis and learned she had less than three months to live, she went to the pond for the last time. She was too weak to go herself, so she asked her daughter, Selina, to take her.

"Take me for a walk, dear," she said, and though the hour was late, Selina, always the dutiful daughter, obliged.

When Janet's wheelchair rolled to a stop beside that timeless body of water, all the troubles of life fell away as they always had. She asked to be left alone, and when her daughter reluctantly stepped away, Janet gazed down at the reflected stars dusting the pond's surface.

She felt the heft of the cosmos—of space and time—bearing down on her with a weight she hadn't felt before. Death would take her soon, and she was scared.

"I wish to soar among the stars."

She threw a quarter into the water. Satisfied that the pond had heard, she called to her daughter and said she was ready to go home.

Five weeks later, Janet coughed up blood. By week seven, she was curled up in bed, a skeleton with paper-thin skin tethered to a morphine pump.

Janet was alone the night she breathed her last. Selina would sit with her for hours at a time, but it was late and Selina had fallen asleep upstairs. At any rate, it wouldn't have made a difference. Hopped up on morphine, Janet drifted through a cloud of dreams a thousand miles away.

Time had dissolved, reducing her life to a series of superimposed snapshots. Underpinning her death dream were memories of her trips to the pond. In her mind, she could hear the same request repeated over and over again.

"I wish to soar among the stars."

As life waned, as death hung over her like a dark shroud, she at last heard the pond's answer, words she'd waited to hear her entire life.

Come, Daughter. It's time for your wish to come true.

There was a slip, a tear, and then Janet's soul rocketed from her body into the cosmos beyond.

Walker

Damon Scott stepped forward, and the world shifted. The trees of the forest fell away to the skyscrapers of a vast city. The last world had been dry, but here it was raining, and he hunched his shoulders and drew into himself as he passed through the city's warren of cold indifferent streets.

He was a walker, like his father, like his grandfather before him. He straddled the narrow but infinite space between the worlds, a cosmic vagrant in search of his lost ancestral home. Nobody could remember where they'd come from or how they'd gotten lost, only that life for the Scott family was one of profound sadness, of longing for a forgotten ideal, of searching for the unknown through countless generations with the blind hope that one day they would find peace in the unknown.

He felt it now, the longing, the sense that what he was searching for was out there, tugging at him as if he were a dog on a long, cosmic leash. It taunted him sometimes, that unknown home; it called out to him when he was at his most vulnerable, parading itself in the shadows, where it always remained just out of sight. "Come to me," it seemed to say, "if you can."

After a time, Damon felt the familiar surge of energy building up inside his chest, a bright and glowing warmth that had begun to spread through his entire body. He could feel it crackling, getting ready to discharge. A footstep. The warmth intensified. A footstep. The warmth became a searing fire. A footstep. Sparks discharged before Damon's eyes. A footstep.

The world shifted and fell away to someplace new.

Who Am I?

GERALD GAZED INTO the Oracle's luminous, pale eyes and asked his question.
"Who am I?"

A feral smile spread across her lips.

"I don't know."

Gerald did his best to remain calm. The Oracle had a reputation for being difficult, but, when pressed, she always told the truth. She lay on a dusty mattress in the far right corner of an abandoned apartment, where a bare bulb hung from the ceiling by a metal chain. It gave no light, only reflected the preternatural blue of the Oracle's eyes.

"No tricks. I've earned my right to ask. Tell me what I want to know."

She was bound by ancient edicts to answer any single question, and among those who knew of her, an audience with the Oracle was the most sought-after prize on Earth. But few managed to track her down. Gerald himself had begun his quest more than five hundred years ago.

Of course, five hundred years was small change when stacked against the millennia in which he'd lived. He'd existed for so long that his origins were a mystery, even to himself. That was why he sought the Oracle's counsel. As a shape-shifter, he'd donned other forms the way a lawyer dons different suits, stealing identities, annexing other people's lives. He'd worn so many faces for so many centuries that his true self, the soul behind the mask, had been lost.

"I said I don't know," and the light in the Oracle's eyes dimmed. "I've answered truthfully, now leave me alone."

"How can you not know?"

It was a universally accepted truth that the Oracle knew everything. Dread kindled in Gerald's heart, but he stood his ground.

"I won't leave without an answer."

The woman on the mattress leaped to her feet, irises flashing in the semi-darkness.

Gerald took an involuntary step back.

"All right," she hissed. "Do you want the *whole* truth?"

Gerald didn't like the way she'd said that, and suddenly he was afraid. He thought that when his quest for the Oracle ended, so too would his quest to find himself. Now he began to doubt. Still, if there was anyone who could tell him what he wanted to know, it was the Oracle.

"Yes," he said, steeling himself for whatever she would say next. "The whole truth. All of it."

The Oracle flashed him a predatory grin.

"I don't know," she said, "because there's nothing left that makes you *you*. Your entire life has been an imitation of others. You take the forms of those around you so you can blend in, because it's safe, because by being like everyone else, you can avoid the persecution reserved for those who are different.

"But your quest for security came at a cost. You sacrificed your identity and gave up everything that made you who you are. When I look at you now, I see only vanity and affectation. That's why I say, *I don't know who you are.*"

She had to be lying.

But the Oracle didn't lie.

There had to be something that set him apart, something he could claim as his own. He closed his eyes to think. A name, a place, a habit, anything that made him unique. Like beads on a string, he traced through his various forms for as far back as he could remember. But by the time he reached the end of the string, there was only a void in place of memory, an impenetrable darkness that wouldn't allow him to go back any further.

"I have peered into your soul," proclaimed the Oracle, "and have found only emptiness. It would be better if you had died."

"Liar!"

Gerald looked up to confront her, to demand another answer. But the Oracle was gone.

Afterword

I hope you enjoyed (and will continue to enjoy) this compilation. The stories inside, along with their introductions, all contain pieces of myself I don't ordinarily feel comfortable sharing with others. It's not easy to bare your soul for the world to see. You have no idea how people are going to react: if they're going to embrace you as one of their own, or shunt you out into the cold dark of night to stand before the window, forced for the rest of your days to look in from the outside.

Yet as terrifying as revealing the complexities of my heart might be, my need to climb to the highest rooftop and proclaim, "I'm here, and this is who I am," will always be greater. Writing is a great personal risk, especially during such troubling times, when people are so deeply divided and when people can find reason to take offense at almost anything. But the only thing worse than failing is to look back at the end of your life and realize you never tried, that you never gave yourself the chance to succeed. I might fail, perhaps today, perhaps tomorrow—perhaps one, five, or even ten years down the road. But I refuse to look back on my life as a bitter old man, wondering how things could have been different, if only I hadn't been afraid to try.

I'm going to take one small risk right now by ending with a quote. Ending with a quote is the most clichéd thing in the world to do, but this so beautifully encapsulates what I'm trying to say about the difficulty of writing, and I have to share it.

"There is nothing to writing. All you do is sit down at a typewriter and bleed."
—Ernest Hemingway[3]

---

[3] This probably wasn't actually said by Hemingway. It's a convenient attribution, but after some quick searching online to verify the source, I found this: **https://quoteinvestigator.com/2011/09/14/writing-bleed/**

About the Author

Jeff Coleman's passion for storytelling goes all the way back to third grade, when he wrote his first (not very good) short story about a leprechaun who enjoys eating green food. While growing up, he was captivated by classic Nintendo games like Zelda, and later computer games like Myst, each of which took place in worlds very unlike our own, and set his imagination aflame with possibilities for his own tales.

During his college years, Jeff fell in love with math, physics and philosophy, subjects that seeded his heart with a profound interest in the many extraordinary mysteries to be found in apparently ordinary things. Jeff is a firm believer that there is more to the universe than immediate appearances suggest, that there is more to our existence than meets the eye. He's therefore fascinated by stories which probe beyond surface observations, stories which attempt to explore the strange and preternatural, stories which unsettle us, which make us think, which make us question what we are and why we're here.

Some of his favorite books are "The Dark Tower," by Stephen King; "Neverwhere" and "American Gods," by Neil Gaiman; "The Night Circus," by Erin Morgenstern; "The Golem and the Jinni," by Helene Wecker; and "Harry Potter," by J.K. Rowling.